Spartan + Friends
I0729978

To every young soul who dreams of horses, hold fast to that spark.

Never stop reaching, never stop believing, and never let anyone tell you it won't happen. Go to your local riding school, roll up your sleeves, and do the hard work. Offer your hands and heart just to be near the horses, because every moment with them is a step closer to your dream.

Dreams are not built in a single day, they are shaped in sweat and hope, in patience and persistence. Each gate you open, each stall you muck, each lesson you earn brings you nearer to the life you imagine.

I know, because I was once that child, wishing with all my heart to belong in the world of horses. And today, I stand beside Spartan, my heart horse, my dream come true. May you find your own Spartan one day.

# Chapter 1

Hazel skipped across the gravel yard, her boots crunching on the stones. The air smelled of hay and that beautiful damp tree scent left behind by the gentle rain that had pattered on her window as she slept last night. Puddles still glistened on the driveway, and the gum trees around the paddocks dripped with tiny beads of water. Somewhere in the distance, a kookaburra's laugh rang out, loud and cheerful, as if it too was excited for the day ahead.

Hazel breathed it all in. She couldn't help smiling, every visit here felt like stepping into her own secret world, a place filled with horses, friends, and adventures waiting to happen.

As she made her way down the long stable row, she peeked into the stalls, calling out greetings. Dot, the golden Palomino Quarter Horse, lifted her head from her hay net, her soft eyes blinking sleepily. "Morning, Dot,"

Hazel whispered, stroking the mare's nose before moving on.

In the next stall, a boy about her age was adjusting a rug on his pony. Hazel didn't know him very well yet. He had only started lessons a few weeks ago, but she gave him a small smile and a wave. He nodded shyly before disappearing behind his pony's broad rump. Hazel's curiosity flickered, but she didn't stop to talk. She had lots to do before her lesson and she didn't want to be late.

Further along, the sound of squeaking leather and clanging buckles drifted through the yard as other riders tightened girths and checked bridles. A couple of the older girls laughed together as they brushed mud off their horses' legs. The whole yard buzzed with its morning rhythm, hooves stamping, hay rustling, and children chattering.

At the far end of the stables stood the horse Hazel loved most in the whole world: Spartan. He was a Friesian, tall and proud, with a coat as dark as midnight and a mane that tumbled over his neck like long waves of silk. Even standing quietly in his stall,

Spartan looked like a king among horses. Hazel's Aunt Becky always said Spartan looked as though he'd stepped out of a fairytale, and Hazel agreed.

"Morning, Spartan," Hazel whispered as she slid the bolt on his stable door. His kind brown eyes blinked at her, and he let out a soft whinny that warmed her heart. Hazel loved it when he greeted her this way. It made her feel so special, like Spartan was just as excited to see her.

She reached up with her brush and began grooming. Each stroke made his coat shine, and the dust floated away in little clouds in the sunlight streaming through the stable window. Spartan shifted his weight, leaning ever so slightly into the brush. Hazel giggled.

"You're such a big baby sometimes," she told him, scratching his chest where he liked it best.

Becky wasn't Hazel's aunt in the strictest sense, she was Omie's cousin, but she had always been "Aunt Becky" to Hazel. On lesson days, Aunt Becky kindly let Hazel ride

Spartan, and in return Hazel helped to look after him.

Hazel worked carefully, moving around Spartan the way Aunt Becky had taught her. Grooming wasn't just about making Spartan look pretty, it was about keeping him healthy, brushing away dirt and checking for any bumps or cuts. Aunt Becky often reminded Hazel that not every child is lucky enough to ride, and how important it is to do all the chores to look after Spartan as well as the fun things. Hazel never minded. She loved the quiet rhythm of brushing, the way Spartan seemed to sigh happily, and the pride she felt when he gleamed from nose to tail.

Still, as much as Hazel loved her aunt's horse, she had a dream of her own. *One day, I'll have my very own horse,* she thought as she brushed down his strong shoulder. *One that's mine to look after, mine to ride, mine to love forever.*

She ran her hand down Spartan's leg, and he lifted his hoof up for her, waiting for her to pick it clean. Hazel balanced the heavy foot in her hand and smiled. "You're the best helper, you know that?"

From the next stall over, came a loud snort. Chester, the cheeky black-and-white Gypsy Cob, shoved his nose over the door, his whiskers twitching as though to say, *have you got any treats today?* Hazel laughed.

"Morning to you too, Chester. You'll have to wait til later!"

Down the row, Dot gave another soft nicker, and a young bay gelding pawed at his bedding as if impatient for breakfast. Hazel grinned. She loved the way each horse had their own voice and quirky personality.

When Spartan was shining from head to tail, Hazel fetched his saddle. She grunted as she lifted it, Spartan was tall, and she had to stand on her tiptoes to swing it onto his back. He stood perfectly still, like he always did, as though he knew Hazel was only just tall enough to reach.

"Good boy," Hazel puffed, tightening the girth strap. "You make it easy for me."

Just then, Aunt Becky's voice floated across the yard. "How are you going there, Hazel?"

"Almost done!" Hazel called back proudly.

Aunt Becky appeared at the stable door, her hands full of hay nets. Her hair was tied back under a cap, and strands of straw clung to her jumper. "Looks like he'll shine brighter than the sun with all that brushing. You've done an awesome job."

Hazel's cheeks glowed. "Thanks, Aunt Becky. He likes it when I scratch his chest."

"I'm sure he does," Aunt Becky said with a smile. "Don't forget to check your girth is tight before you ride and pop your helmet on. Safety first."

Hazel nodded seriously. Aunt Becky never let her forget that safety was just as important as fun.

With the girth tightened and his bridle buckled, Hazel led Spartan out into the morning light. The yard was alive now, other children were leading their horses to the arena, their voices full of excitement. Parents stood nearby with cameras or mugs of hot coffee, watching proudly. Hazel waved to her mum sitting in the shade. Her dad was at work today, he was a police officer, so he couldn't always make it to watch her whole ride, but Hazel knew he would likely swing by later.

The gum trees swayed gently in the breeze, their branches whispering like they too were eager for the day's lessons to begin.

Hazel paused for a moment, resting her cheek against Spartan's warm shoulder. "Someday, I'll have a horse of my own," she whispered. "But you will always have a place in my heart. I'll still help Aunt Becky to take the best care of you."

Spartan flicked an ear back, as if he understood every word. Hazel liked to believe he did.

She mounted, settling into the saddle. Spartan shifted his weight as she found her balance, patient as always. The yard stretched out before her, alive with the clink of buckles, the laughter of riders greeting one another, and the steady thump of hooves.

Hazel breathed in deeply. The smell of damp grass, warm horses, and fresh hay filled her lungs. She was in her happy place, and she couldn't wait for today's lesson to begin.

With a gentle squeeze of her legs, Spartan stepped forward, his hooves ringing with her favourite sound—click, clack—on the gravel. Hazel's heart gave a flutter of excitement. Whatever today's lesson held, she and Spartan were ready.

# Chapter 2

Spartan's steady hooves carried Hazel across the yard toward the arena. The morning sun peeked out from behind drifting clouds, lighting the puddles like silver mirrors. The smell of wet earth mixed with the tang of leather and the sweet scent of hay. Hazel sat a little taller in the saddle, proud to be riding such a magnificent horse.

The arena gates were wide open, and children were already gathering inside. Some led their ponies around on loose reins to warm up, while others sat waiting in the saddle, swinging their legs and chatting to friends. Hazel's eyes flickered across the line of horses: tall, small, dappled, sleek. Each one had its own spark.

She guided Spartan through the gate, giving a polite nod to Miss Laura, the instructor, who stood at the centre of the arena with her clipboard. Miss Laura was kind but firm, the

sort of person who could spot a loose girth or crooked stirrup from a mile away.

"Good morning, Hazel," Miss Laura called, her voice carrying easily across the sand. "Spartan looks beautiful today."

Hazel beamed. "Thank you!" She'd spent extra time brushing him, and it felt wonderful to have someone notice.

She steered Spartan to one side, letting him walk on a loose rein. His ears flicked forward and back, listening to every sound in the arena. Hazel breathed deeply and let herself relax into his steady stride.

Nearby, a cheerful chestnut pony flicked its tail as its rider, a boy with freckles and a wide grin trotted past. Hazel recognised him as Oliver, one of the other regular riders.

"Hi, Hazel!" he called, bouncing happily in the saddle.

"Hi!" Hazel replied, lifting a hand in greeting.

She loved how friendly most of the riders were. Already she could see two girls on matching ponies giggling as they tried to balance with their arms stretched out like aeroplane wings. Miss Laura gave them a quick warning look, and they straightened up immediately, stifling their laughter.

But not everyone was laughing. At the far end of the arena, a tall grey Warmblood gelding moved with smooth, floating strides, his mane braided neatly along his neck. His rider, Grace, sat tall and perfect in the saddle, her polished boots glinting in the sunlight. She didn't spare a glance for anyone else as she guided Maverick in a graceful circle.

Hazel swallowed. Maverick really was stunning, and Grace always made sure everyone knew it. She remembered Grace boasting once that Maverick had been trained by "the best trainers' money could buy."

Hazel stroked Spartan's neck and whispered, "You don't need the best trainers' money can buy, boy. You're perfect just the way you are."

And she meant it. Spartan had been trained by Aunt Becky, guided by Miss Laura, and his education was about connection, trust, and being safe out on trail rides where anything could happen. Spartan was sure-footed and brave, there was no way Aunt Becky would let Hazel ride him otherwise.

As more riders gathered, Hazel spotted the shy boy she'd passed earlier in the stables. He was leading a small grey pony into the arena. Hazel blinked. No, it wasn't just small. It was tiny compared to the larger horses the other children were riding. The little pony had a spotted rump and pricked ears, its cheeky eyes glinting as though it was planning mischief.

The boy swung himself into the saddle with practiced ease. Hazel smiled to herself. She hadn't spoken to him yet, but she had a feeling she would soon.

Miss Laura clapped her hands. "All right, riders! Walk your horses around the outside of the arena, nice long reins and soft hands. Let's get warmed up. And remember, keep a safe distance between you and the horse in front."

The group shuffled into line. Hazel guided Spartan behind Oliver's chestnut pony, keeping a careful gap between them. Around

and around the arena they went, the sound of hooves drumming a steady rhythm on the sand. The air filled with soft squeaks of saddles, the swish of tails, and the occasional snort from a restless pony.

"Eyes up, everyone," Miss Laura reminded. "Heels down. Think tall in your saddle."

Hazel lifted her chin and rolled her shoulders back. Spartan's walk was powerful yet smooth, and she felt proud sitting on him. Each stride seemed to say, *we've got this.*

She risked another glance around the arena. The freckled boy Oliver was chatting easily to the rider beside him. The giggling girls were now focused, their ponies trotting politely. Grace and Maverick continued their perfect, floating circles, Grace's nose tipped ever so slightly in the air. And the boy on the tiny spotted pony? He was concentrating hard, keeping the little horse in line, though the pony's ears flicked this way and that as though she might bolt into trouble at any moment.

Hazel's heart swelled. The laughter, the shining coats, the mix of horses and ponies—

all of it wrapped around her like a warm blanket.

This was more than just a lesson. This was a yard full of horses and maybe, just maybe, the start of new friendships.

"Change direction across the diagonal!" Miss Laura called.

Hazel gathered her reins and gently squeezed with her legs. Spartan stepped forward, his long stride eating up the sandy track. She guided him carefully across the arena, keeping her eyes up just as Miss Laura had taught her.

"That's it, Hazel," Miss Laura encouraged. "Nice straight line. Look where you're going, not down at his mane."

Hazel's cheeks flushed. She quickly lifted her gaze toward the opposite corner. Spartan was such a steady horse that sometimes she forgot her riding mattered too. But when she gave him the right signals, he responded instantly, like the two of them were having a quiet conversation only they could hear.

Around her, the arena bustled with the rhythm of horses moving in different directions. Hooves crunched in the sand, and riders concentrated on their tasks.

 "Prepare to trot!" Miss Laura called. "Rise and fall with the movement. Don't forget your diagonals!"

Hazel took a deep breath. She shortened her reins and gave Spartan a gentle squeeze with her calves. He lifted into trot, his stride smooth and powerful beneath her. Hazel began rising and sitting in rhythm, her body moving like she'd practiced so many times.

"Good job, Hazel!" Aunt Becky called from the sideline, giving her a little wave. Hazel's heart lifted. Even with so many riders in the arena, Aunt Becky always seemed to notice her.

Oliver whizzed past on his chestnut pony, grinning from ear to ear. "Race you to the end!" he teased, though he was already halfway there.

Hazel laughed. "No fair—you started first!"

Miss Laura's sharp whistle cut through the air. "Oliver, no racing. Back in line, please."

Oliver slowed his pony sheepishly, though his grin didn't fade.

At the far end, Grace nudged Maverick into canter, even though Miss Laura hadn't asked for it. The grey Warmblood surged forward in a floating stride that turned heads. Grace sat tall, her hands perfectly still, as if she were riding in a show ring instead of a group lesson.

"Grace," Miss Laura's voice was firm, "please keep to the exercise. Trot only for now."

Grace slowed Maverick back to trot but not before flashing a smug smile at the other riders. "He just loves to canter," she said sweetly.

Hazel's stomach twisted. She knew Grace was showing off, but part of her wished she could look as polished and effortless. Then she reminded herself: Spartan wasn't trained to win ribbons or impress judges. He was trained to keep her safe, to be brave on trails, to look after her. That meant more than fancy circles.

Spartan tossed his head gently, and Hazel leaned forward to pat his neck. "You're all I need," she whispered. His ears flicked back toward her as if in agreement.

"Now, everyone, bring your horses back to walk," Miss Laura called. "We'll set up for a little exercise with the cones. Bending lines, one at a time."

Hazel slowed Spartan, feeling proud that she'd managed her trot without losing balance. She glanced across the arena again. The shy boy on the spotted pony sat quietly, guiding his tiny mount with gentle hands. Hazel wondered what his name was. He looked like someone she'd like to know.

Miss Laura walked toward the line of bright orange cones set out in the middle. "Remember," she said, raising her voice so they all could hear, "it's not about going the fastest. It's about accuracy. Keep your turns neat, use your outside leg, and guide your horse with soft hands."

Hazel's chest fluttered with excitement. Spartan was good at bending exercises, and she loved weaving through cones like a dance. She sat tall, waiting for her turn, her eyes sparkling as the first rider trotted into the pattern.

This wasn't just a warm-up anymore. It was the start of real riding and Hazel was ready to show what she and Spartan could do.

# Chapter 3

Hazel watched as Oliver guided his chestnut pony neatly through the cones, his grin wide as ever. The pony's ears flicked back and forth, listening, but Oliver's hands were steady, and the pair finished the exercise with a smooth turn back to the line of waiting riders.

"Very nice, Oliver," Miss Laura praised. "Next!"

One by one, each rider took their turn. Some ponies shuffled sideways or cut corners, and one got distracted by the hedge outside the arena, but Miss Laura encouraged them all.

When it was Hazel's turn, she gave Spartan a gentle nudge with her outside leg and steered him toward the first cone. His long stride carried them smoothly into the pattern. Hazel focused on keeping her hands soft, her eyes up, just like Miss Laura always reminded her. Spartan bent around each

cone with ease, his black mane rippling as he turned.

"Lovely, Hazel," Miss Laura said. "See how he listens when you give clear signals?"

Hazel's heart swelled with pride. She gave Spartan's neck a grateful pat as they rejoined the line.

Then Miss Laura called, "And now… Huxley, your turn."

Hazel's ears pricked at the name. *So that's what his name is,* she thought, watching as the shy boy she'd noticed in the stables nudged his tiny grey Appaloosa forward.

Suki trotted toward the cones, her spotted rump swinging side to side with more energy than direction. The little mare tossed her head, clearly unimpressed with the idea of weaving neatly.

"Steady, Suki," Huxley murmured, his voice calm.

The pony darted around the first cone, skipped sideways at the second, then decided it was much more interesting to try and nibble at the third. The watching riders burst into laughter. Even Hazel couldn't help but giggle behind her hand.

But what struck her wasn't the pony's cheekiness, it was Huxley. He didn't yank at the reins or grow frustrated. He sat patiently, gently guiding Suki back on track. "Come on, girl, we can do this," he encouraged, as if he had all the time in the world.

They finished the course in their own wobbly fashion, and Huxley gave Suki a fond pat on the neck as though she'd just won a prize.

"Well done for keeping calm, Huxley," Miss Laura said with approval. "That's good horsemanship. Sometimes it's not about perfection, but about patience."

Hazel felt her cheeks warm. She liked the way Miss Laura praised him, not for control or style, but for kindness.

As the group began walking their horses around the arena again, Hazel found herself alongside Huxley and Suki. She smiled nervously. "She's… very fast for such a little pony."

Huxley grinned, a dimple appearing on his cheek. "Yeah. She thinks she's as big as a Clydesdale. Doesn't like being told what to do, either."

Hazel laughed. "She's funny. What's her name?"

"Suki," Huxley replied, patting the pony's spotted neck. "She can be a bit naughty, but I don't mind. She keeps things interesting."

Hazel glanced at Spartan, tall and gleaming beside tiny Suki. "I think they'll get along," she said softly.

For the first time that morning, Huxley looked straight at her, his shy smile brightening. "Yeah. Maybe we will too."

Hazel felt something flutter inside her chest. She didn't know it yet, but this was the beginning of a friendship that would change everything.

The lesson wound down with the riders weaving one last time through the cones, then circling on a long rein to cool their horses down. The sun had climbed higher now, breaking through the last of the clouds and warming the damp sand beneath their hooves.

"Good work today, everyone," Miss Laura called. "That's enough for now, please dismount and loosen your girths."

Hazel swung down from Spartan, landing lightly on the sand. She loosened his girth a hole and rubbed his neck, whispering, "Good boy. You were amazing." Spartan lowered his head, blowing warm air into her hands.

Nearby, Huxley slid off Suki. The little mare immediately tried to snuffle at the edge of the arena fence in search of grass. Hazel giggled. "She never stops, does she?"

"Nope," Huxley replied, tugging gently on her reins. "Food first, rules later. That's Suki's motto."

As Hazel led Spartan out of the arena, she spotted her mum waiting by the fence. Her mum waved, her smile warm and proud.

"You sat beautifully in that trot today," Mum said. "I could see you rising in time with Spartan's steps. Much smoother than when you first started."

Hazel's eyes lit up. "You noticed?"

"Of course I noticed," Mum said with a wink. "I might not ride as much as Aunt Becky anymore, but I still remember what it feels like. I used to be able to keep up with her on trail rides, you know."

Hazel grinned. She'd heard the stories of her mum and Aunt Becky riding through the bush together, having more adventures than Mum liked to admit.

Mum reached up to stroke Spartan's velvety nose. "And this boy, he's such a steady horse. The kind you can trust."

Hazel nodded proudly. "He really is."

Just then, Huxley led Suki past. Hazel cleared her throat. "Mum, this is Huxley. And… this is Suki."

Huxley shifted shyly but managed a polite, "Hello."

Mum's eyes softened as she looked at the pony's spotted rump. "Well, isn't she a character. She looks like she's got plenty of personality."

Huxley's smile widened, the dimple showing again. "She does. She keeps me on my toes."

Mum chuckled. "The best ponies usually do. You two look like a good match." She glanced between Hazel and Huxley, her eyes kind. "And Hazel, it's nice to see you riding alongside someone your own age. You'll have more fun that way."

Hazel's cheeks glowed, and she bent her head as if to fuss with Spartan's reins. But inside, she felt a warm glow of happiness.

Back at the stables, Hazel and Huxley tied up their horses side by side. Hazel pulled the saddle off Spartan's back with a grunt, while Huxley untacked Suki, who immediately tried to snatch mouthfuls of hay from a nearby net.

"Stop that," Huxley said, tugging her gently away.

Hazel laughed. "She's cheeky."

"She's hungry," Huxley corrected with a grin. "Always."

They worked in companionable silence for a while, brushing down their horses. Hazel loved the sound of the bristles sweeping through Spartan's glossy coat, the earthy scent of horsehair and dust rising around them. Out of the corner of her eye, she noticed Huxley's steady movements, calm, patient, not rushed. It made her think again of how he'd handled Suki in the arena.

When Spartan was tidy, Hazel pulled an apple from her pocket. She split it in half and offered one piece to Spartan, who crunched it happily. Then, with a small, nervous smile, she held out the other half to Huxley.

"Do you want this for Suki?"

Huxley blinked in surprise before his smile returned, slow and warm. "Thanks." He took the apple and held it flat on his palm. Suki's lips tickled his hand as she gobbled it up, leaving a smear of juice. Huxley wiped it on his jeans, laughing.

Hazel laughed too. The sound mingled with the rustle of horses eating and the chatter of children in the yard. For the first time, she realised she wasn't just happy because of

Spartan. She was happy because she had someone new to share it all with.

# Chapter 4

The next Saturday dawned crisp and bright, the kind of morning where the sky stretched wide and blue over the paddocks. Hazel hummed to herself as she brushed Spartan's silky mane, her excitement bubbling. Today Miss Laura had promised a "games day" in the arena, an idea that had sent all the riders buzzing.

By the time Hazel led Spartan through the arena gate, the cones, poles, and a set of bright plastic buckets were already laid out. Miss Laura stood in the centre, her whistle dangling on a string around her neck.

"Good morning, riders!" she called. "Today we're going to practise balance, steering, and control… but in the form of games."

A cheer rose from the younger riders. Even Spartan pricked his ears forward as if curious.

Hazel lined up beside Oliver, who was chatting about how his pony was "definitely going to win." On her other side, Huxley sat quietly on Suki, giving the little mare a reassuring pat as she tossed her head. Hazel offered him a grin, and he gave a small one back.

"First up will be the egg and spoon race!" Miss Laura announced. She walked along the line, handing each rider a plastic spoon with a small ball balanced on top. "You'll ride at walk only. If you drop the ball, you go back to the start. Ready?"

Hazel tightened her grip on the reins and tried to balance the ball at the same time. Spartan shifted beneath her, steady but powerful. *Easy, boy,* Hazel thought. *Slow and smooth wins the race.*

"Go!" Miss Laura blew the whistle.

Ponies plodded forward, riders wobbling as they tried to keep their spoons steady. Giggles broke out almost immediately as Oliver's ball tumbled into the sand. "Oh, come on!" he groaned, circling back to the start.

Hazel focused hard, her tongue sticking out slightly as she kept the spoon level. Spartan's calm walk carried her steadily down the track. Out of the corner of her eye, she noticed Huxley, Suki was trotting cheekily despite his steady hands, his ball flew off in seconds. Instead of frowning, Huxley laughed and gave Suki's neck a pat.

At the far end, Grace and Maverick glided along as though they were in a parade, Grace's spoon held perfectly still. She looked down the line at the others, smirking. "This is hardly a challenge."

Hazel clenched her jaw but kept her eyes on the finish line. Step by steady step, Spartan carried her across without dropping the ball.

"Well done, Hazel!" Miss Laura praised. "That's control and focus."

Hazel's cheeks glowed. She'd beaten Grace, not because Spartan was perfect, but because he was steady, and she'd stayed calm.

"Right," Miss Laura called. "The next game will be red light, green light!"

Excited whispers broke out as she explained the rules. The riders would trot toward her when she called "green light" and halt immediately at "red light." The last to stop would go back to the start.

Hazel gathered her reins, her heart thumping with anticipation. Spartan pawed the ground, eager for the cue.

"Green light!" Miss Laura shouted.

The line of horses surged forward, sand flying. Hazel rose into her trot, feeling Spartan's smooth rhythm beneath her.

"Red light!"

Hazel sat deep and closed her hands. Spartan stopped squarely in an instant. Giggles echoed as Oliver's pony slid a few extra steps, and Suki spun sideways before halting, ears flicking mischievously.

"Good, Hazel," Miss Laura said. "Excellent stop."

Hazel patted Spartan's neck proudly. She glanced sideways at Huxley, who shrugged good-naturedly as Suki pawed at the ground,

clearly annoyed the game wasn't about running full speed. Hazel giggled.

As the games went on there were sack races, bending poles, and weaving between cones, the arena rang with laughter and cheers. Even the shyest riders joined in, their ponies picking up on the excitement. Grace still rode with her nose in the air, Maverick perfect in every round, but Hazel didn't care. For once, she wasn't comparing herself. She was just having fun with Spartan, and with new friends by her side.

When the lesson ended, the riders dismounted, flushed and smiling. Miss Laura clapped her hands together. "That's enough for today! Remember, games are fun, but they're also about practising your balance, coordination, and partnership with your horse. You all did brilliantly."

Hazel gave Spartan a big hug around his neck. His coat was warm and damp with sweat, but she didn't mind. "You were amazing bud," she cooed.

Huxley came over, leading Suki, who still looked bright-eyed and cheeky. "She cheated in every game," he said with a grin. "But I think she enjoyed herself."

Hazel laughed. "So did we."

And as they walked their horses back toward the stables, Hazel felt it again, that happy flutter in her chest. Riding wasn't just lessons anymore. It was fun, it was friendship, and it was the beginning of something bigger than she could have imagined.

They were just about to head toward the stables when Aunt Becky appeared at the arena gate, leading a tall, striking chestnut gelding with splashes of white across his sides. His mane was shorter than Spartan's, his eyes bright and curious. The young horse shifted on his hooves, tossing his head as though the whole world was far too interesting to stand still.

"Hazel, Huxley!" Aunt Becky called. "Would you two like to join me on a short trail ride? Just to cool the horses off?"

Hazel's eyes widened. "Really? Out on the trail?"

"Only a short loop," Aunt Becky said firmly, smiling as Marble nudged her arm with his nose. "Marble here is only three, and he's still very green. I just want to give him a little outing, nothing long. It'll do him good to follow a couple of steady horses."

Before Hazel could answer, another voice chimed in from behind. "That sounds perfect. Dot could use a stretch too."

Hazel turned to see a woman leading Dot, a golden palomino with a flowing cream mane and kind eyes. Dot's hooves clopped neatly on the gravel, her head bobbing as if she knew what was coming.

"This is my mum," Huxley explained quickly, his ears going a little pink. "Dot's hers."

Hazel's grin grew. "Hi! Dot's beautiful."

"She is," Huxley's mum agreed, patting the mare's neck. "I've had her for years. She's steady and clever, a real partner."

Aunt Becky nodded approvingly. "Perfect. Dot will be a good anchor horse for Marble."

Soon, Hazel was mounted on Spartan, Huxley on Suki, Aunt Becky on Marble, and Huxley's mum on Dot. The little group set off down the narrow trail that wound away from the yard, the smell of eucalyptus wrapping around them.

Spartan strode at the front, his ears pricked but calm. Hazel felt proud leading the way. Behind her, Suki pranced to keep up, her spotted rump swinging with cheeky determination. Dot walked steadily with Huxley's mum, her golden coat glowing in the dappled light. Marble, at the back beside Dot, snorted at every fallen branch and rustling bush, his young body buzzing with energy.

"Easy, boy," Aunt Becky murmured, her voice low and steady. "Follow Dot. She'll show you there's nothing to worry about."

Marble flicked an ear toward Dot, as though listening. Hazel smiled over her shoulder. "He's doing really well, Aunt Becky."

"He is," Becky agreed. "This is exactly what he needs, lots of short rides, with calm company."

Huxley chuckled as Suki sidestepped at a noisy black cockatoo that flapped from a branch. "Looks like Marble and Suki agree on scary birds."

Dot, however, walked on without flinching, her golden ears steady. "She's seen it all before," Huxley's mum said fondly, patting her mare's neck. "She's good at keeping everyone else calm."

Hazel grinned at that. It was comforting, knowing Dot belonged to Huxley's family, she had always admired her in the barn. Dot reminded her a bit of her grandmother's horse, Narni's palomino, her name is Biccy, Hazel gets to ride her when she goes for visits.

The four horses moved together down the track, the steady rhythm of hooves mixing with the songs of birds and the creak of saddles. Hazel breathed in the cool, damp scent of gum leaves. She loved the arena, but this, out in the bush, Spartan's stride beneath her, friends around her, felt like freedom.

When the trail looped back toward the yard, Aunt Becky pulled Marble to a halt. The gelding blew out a long breath, finally lowering his head as if admitting the world wasn't so scary after all.

"There," Aunt Becky said softly, stroking his neck. "That's enough for today, Marble. Good boy."

Dot shook her mane, Suki stamped impatiently, and Spartan plodded on as though he could happily walk all day.

Hazel's heart felt light as they headed back toward the stables. Riding Spartan always made her happy, but riding alongside Aunt Becky, Huxley, Huxley's mum on Dot and helping Marble learn, made her feel part of something bigger.

She glanced at Huxley, who was scratching Suki's neck as the little mare marched along, still full of beans. He caught Hazel's eye and grinned. Hazel grinned back.

# Chapter 5

The following week, the yard buzzed with chatter long before the lesson began. Horses stamped in their stalls, the air filled with the squeak of leather and the sweet, dusty smell of hay. Hazel arrived early, brushing Spartan until his coat shone like polished coal.

She couldn't wait to ride with Huxley again. After last week's games and the short trail ride, everything felt different, lighter, happier. For the first time, Hazel had someone her age to share it all with.

When they gathered in the arena, Miss Laura announced, "Today we're practising transitions, walk to trot, trot to canter, and back again. Smoothness and control are the goal."

Hazel sat tall in the saddle, Spartan stepping calmly beneath her. She felt ready.

As usual, Grace was already circling Maverick in a perfect, collected trot. His plaited mane gleamed, and every stride looked effortless.

Hazel tried not to stare, but it was hard. Maverick was beautiful, and Grace knew it any played to all the watching eyes.

"Hazel," Huxley whispered from Suki's back, drawing level with her. "Don't worry. You've got Spartan. He's steady. That's way better than perfect-and-boring over there."

Hazel smothered a giggle. "Don't let Grace hear you say that."

As if on cue, Grace rode closer, Maverick's stride long and smooth. "Are you ready to keep up today, Hazel?" she asked sweetly, though her eyes glinted. "Transitions are a bit tricky if your horse hasn't been trained properly."

Hazel felt her cheeks warm. "Spartan's fine," she said quickly.

Grace gave a light laugh. "Well, I suppose not every horse can be Maverick." She leaned forward to pat his gleaming neck. "He was schooled by a Grand Prix rider last year. He's done everything."

Before Hazel could answer, Miss Laura's voice cut in. "Everyone—trot, then pick up canter at the long side. Ready? Go!"

Hazel tightened her legs, and Spartan moved smoothly into trot. She rose with his rhythm, focusing on her breathing. At the long side, she gave the cue. Spartan lifted into canter, big, bounding strides that made Hazel's heart leap with joy.

"Yes, Hazel!" Miss Laura called. "That's it that was a good transition, keep your balance!"

Hazel smiled, pride bubbling inside her.

Then Grace and Maverick swept past, their canter collected and floating, the picture of elegance. Grace shot Hazel a sideways glance. "See? Easy."

Hazel bit her lip. She knew Maverick was impressive, but she refused to let Grace spoil her moment. She gave Spartan's neck a firm pat. "Good boy. You're perfect to me."

Meanwhile, Huxley was trying to coax Suki into canter. The little mare tossed her head, then zoomed forward in a burst of energy, leaping into the gait like a rocket. Huxley clung on, laughing despite himself as Suki zigzagged across the arena.

Miss Laura's whistle shrilled. "Huxley! Back to the track, control first, speed second!"

"Yes, Miss Laura!" he called, steering Suki back with patience and good humour.

Hazel grinned at him as they passed. "She's got her own ideas, hasn't she?"

"Always," Huxley puffed, giving Suki a pat. "But I'll get her listening. One day."

The lesson moved into sharper transitions. Miss Laura had them trot down the centre line, halt at X, then trot again. Hazel focused hard, feeling Spartan's body respond beneath her. She gave clear signals, and he halted square, then stepped off again without hesitation.

"Well done, Hazel," Miss Laura praised. "That's partnership."

Grace, meanwhile, made a point of halting Maverick with perfect precision, her back straight and her chin high. "He just does everything so easily," she said loudly enough

for the others to hear. Then, glancing at Hazel, she added with a smirk, "It must be nice, riding someone else's horse until you finally get one of your own. If you ever do."

Hazel froze. The words stung more than she expected. She opened her mouth to reply, but no sound came.

Before she could think of something to say, Huxley spoke up. "I think Spartan's amazing," he said simply. "And Hazel rides him really well." His voice wasn't loud, but it carried enough for Grace to hear.

Grace rolled her eyes and urged Maverick into another flawless circle, her braid bouncing against her back.

Hazel blinked at Huxley, gratitude welling in her chest. "Thanks," she whispered.

He shrugged, smiling shyly. "It's true."

Miss Laura blew her whistle, pulling the group back together. "Listen, everyone. It doesn't matter what horse you're on, what matters is how you ride and how you care for them. A horse isn't just about ribbons or fancy moves. It's about trust and partnership."

Hazel sat a little taller, relief washing over her. Miss Laura always seemed to know the right thing to say.

As they cooled their horses down at the walk, Hazel patted Spartan's warm neck. Grace might have her perfect horse and perfect boots, but Hazel knew she had something better, connection.

And now, with Huxley beside her, she had friendship too.

As the riders cooled their horses down, Aunt Becky appeared at the arena gate, Marble dancing lightly at her side. Dot stood quietly beside her, Huxley's mum mounted and smiling.

"Well done, everyone," Aunt Becky called. "We're heading out on a short trail loop to settle Marble. Hazel, Huxley, would you like to come along again?"

Hazel's eyes sparkled. "Yes, please!"

Huxley grinned. "Count us in."

Just then, Oliver trotted up, his freckled face flushed with excitement. "Can I come too? My pony loves the trail!"

Aunt Becky gave a nod. "As long as you listen and keep a safe distance. Spartan will take the lead."

The small group set out: Hazel and Spartan in front, Huxley with Suki close behind, Oliver and his chestnut pony trotting happily at their heels, and Aunt Becky and Huxley's mum bringing up the rear with Marble and Dot. The bush swallowed them quickly, sunlight flickering through gum leaves and the earthy smell of damp bark rising all around.

The trail was alive with sounds, the call of cockatoos overhead, the snap of twigs under hoof, the gentle creak of saddles and the babbling stream in the distance. Hazel breathed it all in. This was her favourite part of riding: the quiet rhythm of horses moving together, the feeling of being part of a herd.

"Spartan's like a train," Oliver called happily from behind. "Nothing scares him!"

Hazel sat a little taller with pride. "He's the best."

Suki darted sideways at a rustle in the undergrowth, and Huxley steadied her gently. "It's just a wallaby, silly girl," he murmured, calm as always.

Dot marched along steadily, ears pricked, while Marble snorted and tossed his head, testing Aunt Becky's patience. "Steady, boy," she soothed. "See? Everyone else is fine."

It felt like the perfect ride. Hazel looked back at Huxley and Oliver, both grinning, and at Huxley's mum and Aunt Becky chatting quietly. She had friends, family, and her beloved Spartan. She couldn't imagine anything spoiling it.

But just outside the arena, hidden behind the hedge, Grace sat on Maverick. Her eyes narrowed as she watched them disappear onto the trail. She had heard Aunt Becky invite Hazel, Huxley, and then Oliver allowed to tag along, but no one thought of her.

"Always Hazel," Grace muttered under her breath. "Always special treatment for the girl who doesn't even have her own horse."

Maverick flicked his ears, shifting impatiently. Grace tightened her reins, her jaw set. "Fine. If they won't invite me, I'll come anyway. And I'll show them that Maverick and I are better than all of them put together."

She nudged Maverick forward, keeping low and quiet, following the group at a distance down the bush track.

Grace's eyes glittered. She had a plan forming, something that would wipe the smiles off Hazel and her friends' faces.

Something that would remind them who really belonged at the top.

# Chapter 6

The trail continued winding gently downhill, gum leaves whispering overhead and the steady beat of hooves echoing through the bush. Hazel sat easy in Spartan's saddle, proud of how calm he was leading the group. Behind her, Suki had settled into an even pace along with Oliver's pony, Suki kept trying to eat the under growth as they ambled along. Marble, although calmer just wouldn't relax.

"You're fine, Marble," Aunt Becky said soothingly. "It's ok bud we've got this."

Hazel turned in her saddle and called back, "Is he going ok back there?"

Aunt Becky gave her a smile. "Yea, we are ok he just needs —"

The words were cut short by the thunder of hooves.

Grace.

She came galloping up the track, Maverick's long strides tearing through the bush. Grace's hair streamed behind her helmet; her boots pressed tight as she urged him faster.

"Grace!" Aunt Becky yelled, her voice sharp with alarm. "Stop! No galloping on the trail!"

But it was too late. Marble's young body tensed at the sudden rush of sound. His ears shot forward, his eyes wide. With a panicked squeal, he reared, front hooves lashing the air.

"Aunt Becky!" Hazel cried.

Marble's sudden leap threw Aunt Becky off balance. She tried to sit deep, but the young gelding twisted beneath her, and she slid from the saddle, landing hard on the ground with a sickening thud.

"No!" Hazel screamed, frozen in her seat.

Aunt Becky groaned, clutching her arm. "I think it might be broken," she hissed through gritted teeth.

Marble spun wildly, eyes rolling, the whites of his eyes flashing. Dot moved away sideways,

Suki planted her feet, and Oliver's pony snorted nervously. The peaceful trail was chaos in seconds.

"Hold your horses steady!" Huxley's mum called, already sliding off Dot. She hurried to Aunt Becky's side. "Don't move, Becky. Keep still we need to make sure your arm is the only thing of concern."

Hazel's hands shook on the reins, but Spartan stood like a statue, his ears flicked back, waiting for her cue.

"Hazel," Aunt Becky gasped, her face pale, "could you take Spartan over to Marble, it will help calm him down."

Hazel swallowed hard, her mind racing. Aunt Becky had often told her how Spartan used to pony Marble as a yearling, teaching him to trust and follow. If anything could calm Marble now, it was Spartan.

"Okay," Hazel whispered, steadying her breathing. She nudged Spartan forward.

The Friesian's calm, powerful presence filled the space between Marble's panic and Hazel's determination. Step by step, Spartan

drew closer, his body relaxed and steady. Marble squealed, sidestepping, but when Spartan reached him, the young gelding's ears flicked forward. Recognition glimmered in his eyes, and he dropped his head just a fraction.

"That's it, Marble," Hazel murmured, reaching out carefully to catch his trailing rein. "It's just us. You know Spartan."

The chestnut quivered, his body taut, but Spartan's calmness anchored him. With Spartan beside him, Marble finally stilled, snorting and then blowing out a long, shaky breath.

"You've got him," Aunt Becky said faintly, relief in her voice. "Good girl, Hazel."

Grace circled Maverick nearby, her face twisted with anger. "This isn't my fault! If you were all better riders, she wouldn't have fallen. Marble's too green for the trail anyway!"

Hazel's stomach clenched, but she didn't answer. She was too focused on Marble, stroking his neck, whispering softly, "Easy, boy. You're safe now."

Huxley dismounted, tying Suki to a tree so he could help his mum with Dot whilst she was with Becky. Oliver slid from his chestnut and stood wide-eyed, clutching his reins.

Hazel took a deep breath. "I can pony him back with Spartan. He'll stay calm beside him."

Aunt Becky nodded, her face pale but determined. "Yes. Walk us back slowly. I'll walk along beside you."

Hazel gathered both sets of reins, Spartan's and Marble's, her hands steady despite her pounding heart. With Spartan guiding, Marble fell into step, still trembling but no longer fighting.

The little group turned back toward the yard and got back on their horses, except for Aunt Becky who was cradling her injured arm walking alongside Spartans shoulder. Hazel rode carefully at the front, Spartan's calm presence easing the tension of the trio,

Marble shadowing his old companion like a lost puppy.

Behind them, Grace scowled, sitting stiffly in Maverick's saddle. She muttered, "Typical. One little fall and everyone acts like it's the end of the world."

Hazel didn't look back. Her only thought was getting Aunt Becky home safe.

As they neared the trail entrance, Miss Laura was waiting, arms folded, her expression sharp with concern. Beside her stood Hazel's mum, her face pale with worry.

The group slowed to a halt. Miss Laura's eyes swept over them, landing on Aunt Becky, who was cradling her arm, then on Hazel holding both Spartan and Marble's reins.

"Goodness, Becky, you're hurt. And Hazel, you've managed both horses?"

Hazel gave a shaky nod, her throat too tight to speak.

Grace sat tall in her saddle, her face flushed. "It wasn't my fault!" she blurted, her voice rising. "Marble just isn't ready for trails, that's all. I was only giving Maverick a stretch, he needs to move out. You can't blame me for Becky falling!"

Miss Laura's eyes narrowed. "We will talk about this later, Grace," she said firmly, her voice leaving no room for argument.

Hazel's mum hurried to Becky's side, she had been waiting for their return ready to take Hazel home. She gently held Becky's injured arm. "We need to get you to hospital for an X-ray. That arm doesn't look good."

Becky tried to brush her off but winced as she moved. "All right, all right. I'll go."

"Good," Mum said, her tone brisk but kind. "I'll drive you straight there." She turned to Hazel. "You can stay here with Spartan. I'll call your dad, so he knows what's happened and to come pick you up. You've done a wonderful job bringing Marble back with Spartan. Are you all right to pop them both away?"

"Of course," Hazel said quickly. "And I'm sure Miss Laura will help me if I need it."

Miss Laura gave a brisk nod. "I'll oversee the horses and riders. Hazel, keep Marble with Spartan until we get him settled in the yard. Everyone else, dismount and walk quietly back."

Hazel squeezed Spartan's reins, guiding Marble close against his side. The young chestnut plodded obediently now, calmer with his old companion beside him.

As her mum led Aunt Becky away toward the car, Hazel's chest tightened. She wanted to go too, but she knew her job was here, with Spartan, with Marble, making sure they were untacked and safe in their stalls.

Behind her, Grace muttered again, her voice small but stubborn. "It wasn't my fault."

Hazel bit her lip. She knew if she retorted Grace would only fight back. And what was the point? Everyone had seen what happened. If Grace hadn't been so careless, none of this would have happened.

# Chapter 7

Hazel led Spartan through the gate with Marble close by his side, the young chestnut shadowing the Friesian's every step. She kept both sets of reins steady in her hands, her heart still thudding from the chaos on the trail. Spartan's calm stride carried them forward, and Marble, trembling but obedient.

The yard was quieter than usual. A few riders were untacking in the wash bay, their chatter fading as they noticed Aunt Becky being helped to the car. Hazel's stomach twisted at the sight, but she forced herself to focus.

"Come on, boys," she whispered. "One step at a time."

She put Spartan into the cross ties after switching his bridle for a halter. Marble snorted and pawed the ground, but Hazel moved him closer to Spartan, and the chestnut settled, his head lowering. Hazel stroked his neck, pride flickering through her nerves.

"You remember this, don't you?" she murmured. "Spartan's looked after you before. He won't let anything bad happen to you."

Miss Laura approached, her expression softening as she watched Hazel work. "You handled that very well, Hazel. Not many riders your age could have kept calm like that."

Hazel ducked her head, her cheeks warm. "Spartan did most of it."

"Spartan was steady," Miss Laura agreed, "but he needed you to guide him. That's good horsemanship—teamwork."

Hazel's chest swelled with quiet pride. She untacked Spartan slowly, brushing the sweat marks from his coat, then turned to Marble. He was younger, fussier, shifting on his feet, but when she kept Spartan close by, Marble sighed and let her run the brush down his shoulder.

Across the yard, Huxley was rubbing down Suki while Oliver filled a water bucket for his chestnut. Both boys kept glancing Hazel's way.

Oliver was the first to speak, his grin wide. "You were amazing out there! I thought Marble was going to bolt, but you… you just had him."

Huxley nodded. "Yeah. Suki would've lost it if Spartan hadn't been so calm. You and he make such a good team."

Hazel smiled shyly, giving Spartan a grateful pat. "Thanks. I just… did what Aunt Becky said to do."

Two girls from their lesson wandered over, curiosity written all over their faces. The taller one had curly brown hair tucked under her helmet, and the other—shorter, with freckles and pigtails—carried a saddle across her arms.

"That was incredible," the taller girl said. "We were still in the arena when we heard shouting. Is Becky all right?"

Hazel nodded. "Mum's taking her to hospital for an X-ray. She hurt her arm, but… I think she'll be okay."

The girl with freckles whistled softly. "And you held Marble? No wonder Miss Laura was praising you. I'd have been terrified."

Hazel's cheeks warmed again. "I was terrified. But Spartan knew what to do."

The taller girl grinned. "Well, it looked brave to us. I'm Sophie, and this is Ella."

Hazel smiled back, feeling the knot in her stomach ease. "I'm Hazel. It seems you already know Huxley and Oliver."

The group exchanged nods and smiles, they all chatted as they worked. Hazel smiled thinking how nice it was to have all these new friends that shared her love of horses.

Across the yard, Grace stood stiffly in front of Miss Laura. Hazel couldn't hear what was being said, but Miss Laura's arms were crossed, her voice sharp and firm. Grace's shoulders hunched lower with every word. Finally, Grace spun on her heel, stormed toward Maverick, and mounted up in a rush. As she wheeled him around, her glare cut straight at Hazel, full of fury, as though Hazel was the reason she'd been scolded.

Hazel looked away quickly, her chest tightening. She didn't want a fight. She just wanted to enjoy the horses.

Moments later, a familiar voice called from the driveway. "Hazel!"

Her dad was there, leaning against the family car, still in his police uniform. Relief flooded Hazel at the sight of him.

She put Spartan and Marble away, giving each a flake of hay and a bucket of fresh water. Hazel pressed a last grateful pat to Spartan's strong neck, then reached out to stroke Marble's soft nose.

Turning to her new friends, she smiled. "See you next week?"

"Definitely," Huxley said, and the others nodded eagerly.

Hazel hurried across the yard, her boots crunching on the gravel, she slipped her hand into her dad's as they headed toward the car, her heart full of questions about what was happening with Aunt Becky.

# Chapter 8

The next afternoon, Hazel sat in the back seat of the car, her stomach knotted as the countryside rolled past the window. She had hardly slept the night before, her head filled with the sound of Marble squealing, the sight of Aunt Becky falling, and the sharp crack of her landing on the ground.

Now, at last, she was on her way to see her.

Her Mum slowed the car outside Becky's little house, Hazel leapt out before the engine had even stopped, clutching the get-well card she had made with colouring pens that morning.

Inside, Aunt Becky was propped up on the couch, her arm in a neat white plaster cast from shoulder to wrist. She still looked pale, but her smile brightened the moment she saw Hazel.

"There's my girl," Aunt Becky said warmly. "Come in, I could use some company."

Hazel rushed forward and perched carefully beside her. "Does it hurt much?" she asked in a small voice.

"Not too much now," Becky replied, shifting slightly. "The doctors gave me something for the pain. I'll be fine, though I won't be lifting hay bales for a while." She gave a wry grin, but Hazel still looked worried.

"I was so scared," Hazel whispered. "If Spartan hadn't been there…"

"Spartan was wonderful," Becky agreed, "but don't forget, Hazel, you were wonderful too. You kept your head and helped Marble settle. I'm proud of you."

Hazel felt her cheeks heat, but she didn't look away. "I only did what you asked me to do."

"That may be true, but you did it calmly and without hesitation, if you had panicked Marble may have bolted and we could still be looking for him." Becky said softly, reaching to squeeze her hand with her good one. "Thank you, Hazel you really did save the day."

Hazel's Mum poked her head out from the kitchen. "She hasn't stopped talking about it," she said with a smile. "She even had me acting out how it all went down."

Hazel groaned. "Mum!"

Becky chuckled. "Well, I'm just glad you were there. You and Spartan made a great team."

Hazel's gaze drifted to the cast on Becky's arm. "How long before you can ride again?"

The smile faded just a little. "A few months, at least. Bones take time, but don't you worry, I'll be back in the saddle before you know it. In the meantime, I might just need an extra pair of hands, are you up to the task?"

Hazel sat up straighter. "Me?"

"Of course, you," Becky said. "Spartan still needs to be looked after, and Marble too. I'll still be able to manage most things, but I might need some extra help during the week too."

Hazel's spirits lifted. She had come expecting to feel helpless, but instead she felt trusted, needed. She leaned gently against Aunt

Becky's good side, the weight of worry easing from her shoulders.

For a moment, they sat quietly, listening to the soft tick of the clock on the mantelpiece. Then Hazel spoke, her voice low but thoughtful.

"Aunt Becky… do you think maybe… I'm ready for my very own horse? I love Spartan, I always will, but after yesterday… it felt like I was really looking after him and Marble."

Becky's eyes softened. She reached across and brushed Hazel's hair back from her face with her good hand. "Hazel, I think you showed more responsibility yesterday than some adults do. Whether it's now or a little later, one day soon, you'll have a horse that's just yours. And when that day comes, I know you'll do right by them."

Hazel's heart fluttered at the words. She could picture it so clearly—a horse she could brush, feed, and ride every day, one that would be hers forever. She smiled and hugged Aunt Becky carefully, her mind full of dreams.

Her Mum jingled the car keys. "Time to head home, Chook. Becky needs her rest."

Hazel stood reluctantly, giving Spartan's photo on the mantel a last glance, then turned back to her aunt. "I'll help at the yard, I promise. You don't have to worry."

"I know," Becky said with a wink. "I've got the best helper in the world."

As Hazel followed her Mum back to the car, the thought of her very own horse stayed with her. Maybe… just maybe… that day wasn't as far away as it used to feel.

# Chapter 9

The week after the accident, the yard felt different. Without Aunt Becky there as much, Hazel felt the weight of responsibility on her shoulders. She arrived straight after school most afternoons, backpack bouncing against her side, ready to help however she could.

Spartan nickered when she appeared, his dark eyes soft. Hazel brushed his gleaming coat until it shone, then checked Marble, who still jumped at sudden noises but calmed whenever Spartan was nearby. Hazel walked the two of them out of their stalls and into a paddock so they could graze. Every step made her feel a little older, a little more capable.

*I am ready,* Hazel thought as she rubbed Marble's white blaze. *Maybe I really could have a horse of my own.*

She often caught herself daydreaming, imagining walking into the yard to see a horse waiting just for her, one she could feed,

groom, and ride whenever she wanted. Sometimes the horse was sleek black like Spartan, sometimes golden like Biccy, sometimes spotted like Suki. But always, it was hers.

One afternoon, Omie came to visit and help Hazel. She leaned against the stable door, her face gentle but her eyes watchful.

"You've grown up a lot this week, Hazel," Omie said softly. "I can see it in the way you handle those horses."

Hazel smiled, though she could see the shadow in her grandmother's eyes. Omie had often said she loved horses but had some bad experiences when she was younger.

"Do you think I'm ready for my own horse, Omie?" Hazel asked.

Omie hesitated, then nodded slowly. "I think you're proving every day that you can take on the work. A horse isn't just about riding, it's about caring for them in all weathers, when it's fun and when it's not. And you've shown you can do that." She reached out and squeezed Hazel's shoulder. "If your parents agree, I'd be happy to contribute to the purchase. You do have a birthday coming up"

Hazel's heart leapt. "You mean it?"

Omie's smile warmed. "I do."

Later that week, Narni came to the yard to help too, wearing her riding boots and carrying a bag of carrots. She kissed Hazel on the cheek before marching straight to Marble's stall.

"Well, aren't you handsome," Narni chuckled, letting Marble lip a carrot from her palm. "He just needs confidence. You'll help him find it."

Hazel led her grandmother out to the paddock, where Spartan grazed peacefully. Narni's eyes softened at the sight of the Friesian. "He is such a beautiful soul."

Hazel leaned against the fence. "Narni… Omie said she'd help if I got my own horse. Do you think… do you think you could help too?"

Narni turned to her with a twinkle in her eye. "Hazel, I've been waiting for the day you

asked me that. Of course I'll help. You have proved you are committed and responsible, I think it is time we start looking for your perfect match."

Hazel's chest swelled with happiness. Both her grandmothers believed in her. Both were willing to help. Suddenly, her dream felt so close she could almost touch it.

That night, as she lay in bed, Hazel hugged her pillow and whispered to herself, "Maybe for my birthday. Maybe soon." She closed her eyes, drifting to sleep with visions of a glossy coat, a soft muzzle, and the sound of hooves carrying her into her very own adventure.

# Chapter 10

The next morning, Hazel padded sleepily into the kitchen, her hair still a tangle from bed. The smell of toast and scrambled eggs filled the air, and sunlight streamed through the window, catching the steam rising from her mum's morning coffee.

Her dad sat at the table, already in his police uniform, buttering toast with one hand while scanning the newspaper with the other. Mum looked up from the stove, smiling. "Morning, Hazel. Hungry?"

"Starving," Hazel admitted, sliding into her chair. But food wasn't the only thing on her mind.

She toyed with her fork for a moment, then finally said, "Mum, Dad… can we talk about something?"

Both parents looked at her with raised eyebrows, waiting. Hazel's heart thumped. "I was thinking… maybe I'm ready for my very own horse."

Her dad's expression softened. "We thought you might bring that up after everything that's happened this week."

Mum sat down across from her, folding her hands. "Hazel, you've shown us how responsible you can be. You kept calm with Marble when Becky was hurt, and you've been helping at the yard every day. We are so proud of you."

Hazel's eyes widened. "So… does that mean yes?"

Her dad chuckled. "It means yes… and no."

Hazel blinked. "What do you mean?"

Mum leaned forward. "Yes, we agree you're ready. You've worked hard, and you've proven you understand that horses are about more than just riding. But…" She paused, searching for the right words. "It must be the *right* horse. Not just the first one we find, or the one that looks pretty. The perfect safe partner for you."

Her dad nodded. "A horse is a big responsibility, Hazel. It's adding another member to the family. We don't want to rush it."

Hazel sat back, thinking. She had dreamed of this moment for so long, her own horse, her best mate. But she knew they were right. Spartan wasn't just beautiful; he was steady, safe, and kind. She needed a horse like that, one she could trust as much as she trusted him.

"I understand," she said quietly. "I don't just want any horse. I want the *right* one too."

Mum reached across the table and squeezed her hand. "Then we're all in agreement. We'll start looking, together. And when we find the right horse, you'll we feel it in your heart."

Hazel's was overcome with hope and excitement. She could barely eat her eggs, her thoughts buzzing with the promise of what lay ahead.

By the time she reached the barn later that morning, her mind was still racing with her parents' words. The yard was unusually busy, riders clustered by the fence, voices buzzing

with excitement. Hazel slowed, curiosity prickling.

"What's going on?" she asked as she spotted Huxley and Oliver leaning against the rail.

"New horse," Oliver said, eyes wide. "Just arrived last night. She's *amazing*."

Hazel slipped in beside them, her eyes drawn to the paddock.

A black mare trotted gracefully across the grass, head high, mane rippling in the breeze. A white star and snip shone on her elegant face, and four perfect white socks flashed with every floating stride. She moved with effortless rhythm, her tail streaming behind her like a banner.

"Wow," Hazel breathed.

"She's a Quarter Horse," Huxley said, his voice almost reverent. "One of the older riders bought her as a new show prospect. They say she's worth a fortune."

The mare arched her neck, striking out with long, springy steps that made the ground seem to tremble beneath her. She was a picture of power and grace, every eye in the yard fixed on her.

Hazel's heart thudded. Part of her longed for a horse like that, so striking, so admired. But as the mare circled the paddock, tail flagging, Hazel thought of Spartan's steady strength and Marble's nervous trust. Flashy was beautiful, yes, but what mattered most was connection.

Still, she couldn't tear her eyes away. "She's gorgeous," Hazel admitted softly.

"Yeah," Oliver agreed with a grin. "Makes me want to ride even more."

Hazel smiled faintly, her mind drifting back to breakfast. Her parents were right. She would wait, not just for a horse that turned heads, but for the one that felt like hers in every way. And until then, she had Spartan, Marble, and her dreams to carry her forward.

# Chapter 11

The arena was alive with energy when Hazel arrived for her lesson. Horses circled on loose reins, riders chatting as they warmed up, and the air hummed with the usual mixture of leather creaks, hoofbeats, and excited voices. But this week, all anyone wanted to talk about was the new mare.

"She's stunning, isn't she?" Sophie said, brushing her hair back under her helmet as she guided her pony in a neat circle. "Did you see her trot in the paddock this morning?"

"Like a dancer," Ella added breathlessly, swinging her legs as her bay gelding plodded along.

Hazel gave Spartan a pat on the neck, pride steadying her excitement. "She's beautiful," she agreed. "But I think she's going to be a lot of work. She looked pretty fiery to me."

Oliver grinned from atop his chestnut pony. "Fiery makes for fun rides."

"Or dangerous ones," Huxley muttered, steadying Suki as she tried to sidestep toward a patch of grass. "Some of us already have enough drama."

The group laughed, the tension of last week's trail ride finally easing.

Then the sound of polished hooves rang against the pathway to the arena. Grace entered, Maverick gleaming as always, his mane in perfect braids. Grace sat tall; her chin lifted.

"Have you all seen the new mare?" she called, loud enough for everyone to hear. "She's a *real* show horse with proper breeding, proper training. Not like some of the other horses here." Her eyes flicked pointedly at Suki and Oliver's chestnut.

Hazel bristled but stayed quiet, running her hand down Spartan's glossy neck. She'd learned by now that Grace wanted a reaction.

Miss Laura's sharp whistle cut across the chatter. "Eyes front, everyone! Warm-up's over. Today we're working on accuracy, straight lines, circles, and keeping your

horses listening to you, not gawking at each other."

The riders moved into a trot, forming a line around the arena. Spartan carried Hazel in his steady rhythm, ears flicking back and forth as she guided him carefully into a twenty-metre circle. He was calm and responsive, his hooves crunching softly in the sand.

"Good, Hazel," Miss Laura called. "Keep your hands steady. Lovely circle."

Hazel beamed, sitting a little taller.

Huxley was next. Suki trotted forward with surprising enthusiasm, trying to cut the circle short. "No, Suki," Huxley said patiently, steering her back on track. Miss Laura nodded approvingly. "Well corrected, Huxley. You didn't let her get away with it."

Grace and Maverick followed, gliding effortlessly into a perfect circle. Grace tilted her head with a little smirk. "Some horses don't need correcting," she said under her breath, just loud enough for Hazel to hear.

Hazel's stomach tightened, but she focused on Spartan, giving him a quiet pat. Deep down the wanted to defend her friend, but now was not the time.

Miss Laura clapped her hands. "All right, now let's ride across the diagonal, make it straight, from letter to letter. No drifting!"

One by one, the riders guided their horses across. Oliver wobbled slightly but corrected in time, Ella's pony cut the corner, and Sophie managed a neat line. Hazel gave Spartan a squeeze and lifted her chin. Together they marched across the diagonal, hooves landing in a beautiful rhythm.

"Yes, Hazel!" Miss Laura called. "That's how it's done."

Hazel's heart lifted.

Grace and Maverick followed with another flawless line, Grace's back stiff and proud. But this time, Maverick tossed his head at the last moment, drifting sideways just enough to lose precision.

Miss Laura's voice was calm but firm. "And Grace, remember even the best horses need

clear direction from their rider. Don't rely on him to do all the work."

Hazel caught the flash of annoyance on Grace's face and quickly looked away, hiding her smile.

As they cooled down at the walk, Sophie rode alongside Hazel. "You know," she said softly, "not everything has to be perfect. I think you and Spartan look really happy together. That's nicer to watch."

Hazel's cheeks warmed. "Thanks. That's what Aunt Becky always says too."

She glanced around the arena at her new friends, Huxley grinning at Suki's antics, Oliver humming as his chestnut plodded along, Ella and Sophie chatting side by side. For the first time, Hazel realised that this group wasn't just about lessons anymore she had made some wonderful friendships, too.

And even though Grace's glare still burned from across the arena, Hazel refused to let it bring her down. She knew she was the lucky one, she had Spartan to ride and the beginnings of great friendships. Grace, with her sour attitude, was only isolating herself. In a way, Hazel almost felt sorry for her, even after everything she had done.

# Chapter 12

After the lesson, Hazel slid from Spartan's back with a satisfied sigh. She loosened his girth and led him to the wash bay, Huxley and Oliver not far behind with Suki and the chestnut pony. Sophie and Ella joined them too, chatting about the lesson as they sponged sweat marks from their ponies' coats.

Hazel ran the brush gently over Spartan's neck, smiling as his eyes softened in contentment. "Good boy," she whispered, pressing her cheek briefly against his glossy shoulder. Marble nickered from his paddock, and Hazel promised herself she'd check on him before she went home.

When the tack was cleaned and the horses settled with hay nets, the children wandered back toward the arena. Their boots scuffed in the sand as they sat along the fence rail, waiting for their parents to arrive. The afternoon sun dipped low, casting golden light across the yard.

Then the sound of hooves rang sharp and quick. Heads turned as one of the older riders appeared, leading the new black Quarter Horse mare. Up close, she was even more striking than she'd been in the paddock. Her sleek coat gleamed, polished to a glow, and the star and snip on her face shone bright against the dark. Four white socks flashed as she pranced lightly beside her rider, her muscles rippling under the saddle.

"She's even prettier close up," Ella whispered, wide-eyed.

The older rider swung smoothly into the saddle, gathered the reins, and guided the mare into the arena. "This is Opal," she called to Miss Laura, who gave a nod of permission. "She's a reining prospect; I thought I'd give her a stretch."

The children leaned forward, barely breathing, as Opal moved into a collected jog, then rolled into a lope as smooth as silk. The rider guided her through spins, the mare's hooves dancing on the spot, then

down into sliding stops that sent sand spraying. The speed, the precision, the sheer grace of it made Hazel's heart race.

"She's amazing," Oliver breathed.

"It's like she's reading her mind," Huxley added, his eyes wide.

Hazel's mouth was dry. She had seen horses work in the arena before, but never like this. Opal and her rider moved as though they were one being, every signal invisible, every movement sharp and perfect.

After a dazzling run of circles, spins, and stops, the mare slowed to a walk. The rider turned her toward the children by the rail. "You've got quite an audience," she said with a laugh, patting Opal's shining neck. "I'm Izzy. And this is Opal, my new girl."

"She's beautiful," Sophie said at once, her voice breathless with awe.

"Thanks," Izzy replied warmly. "She's still pretty young, but she's got the heart for it. Lots of work ahead, though. Horses like her don't get this way overnight." She winked at

Hazel. "Takes years of practice and partnership."

Hazel nodded, her heart fluttering. *Partnership.* That was what she wanted most of all.

Just then, Hazel heard a familiar voice. "Well, would you look at that."

Her mum and Narni had arrived, standing a little behind the group with warm smiles. Mum slipped an arm around Hazel's shoulders. "She's stunning, isn't she?"

Hazel nodded eagerly. "She's incredible. Did you see her spin?"

Narni chuckled. "I saw. Reminds me of the first time I watched a reining horse. They make it look easy, but the hours behind the scenes are what really count."

In the arena, Izzy circled Opal once more, preparing for another run-through. "One more practice," she called, and the mare launched into motion again. The children clung to the fence, Hazel's mum and Narni watching too, as Opal tore across the arena, stopped dead in a shower of sand, and spun like a dancer.

Hazel's chest ached with longing. Watching Opal and Izzy, she couldn't help imagining herself one day in that saddle—not on Opal, but on her own horse. A horse that would trust her, respond to her, and dazzle her friends the way Opal was right now.

She pressed closer into her mum's side. "Someday," Hazel whispered, "I'll have a horse like that. One that's mine."

Her mum smiled softly, kissing the top of her head. "Yes, love. Someday you will."

# Chapter 13

The next afternoon, Hazel skipped across the gravel driveway, her schoolbag bouncing on her back. She had been looking forward to this all day, Narni had promised she might visit today. Hazel's heart leapt when she spotted the familiar car parked by the stables. Even better, a horse trailer gleamed behind it, the sunlight flashing off its silver sides.

Hazel stopped in her tracks, her breath catching. *The trailer!*

"Narni's here!" she gasped, running the last few steps. She slowed only when she reached the trailer door, peeking eagerly through the windows. A soft golden muzzle pressed forward, whiskers twitching, eyes warm and knowing.

"Biccy!" Hazel squealed.

Narni appeared from the tack room at the front of the horse trailer, with a wide smile on her face. "Thought we'd surprise you," she

said, jingling the lead rope in her hand. "Biccy's going to stay here at the barn for a few weeks. I figured we could ride together, especially since Becky is out of action now, what do you think?"

Hazel threw her arms around her grandmother in delight. "Really? You mean it? Oh, Narni, this is the best surprise ever!"

Together they lowered the ramp, and Biccy stepped carefully out. The Palomino's golden coat gleamed, her mane catching the sunlight in creamy waves. Hazel stroked her neck, breathing in that familiar grassy, horsey scent.

"She hasn't changed a bit," Hazel whispered. "She might be getting on in years now, but she looks just as sprightly as ever."

"I think she is pretty excited to be here," Narni said proudly. "And she'll enjoy the company. Spartan will keep her honest, and Marble might even learn a thing or two from watching her."

Hazel laughed, her hand still pressed to Biccy's warm shoulder. "He needs a calm teacher. Maybe Biccy can help him be brave."

As they led Biccy toward an empty stall, Spartan nickered from his stable, his deep voice carrying across the barn. Marble's head popped over the door too, ears pricked. Hazel giggled. "See? They already know someone new's arrived."

Narni clipped Biccy's lead rope to the ring, and Hazel fetched a hay net. It felt so natural, the two of them working side by side, like they had done countless times before.

Once Biccy was settled with fresh hay, Hazel leaned on the door, her heart brimming. "This is going to be the best few weeks ever. We can go on trails, ride in lessons, even just brush our horses together."

Narni chuckled, giving Hazel's braid a gentle tug. "That's exactly what I was hoping for. Riding's fun on your own, but it's even better when you share it."

Hazel nodded, unable to stop smiling. Watching Spartan, Marble, and now Biccy all

under one roof brought a huge smile to her face.

And tucked underneath that joy was a little thought that glowed brighter every day: *Maybe soon, I'll have a horse of my own to join them too.*

# Chapter 14

The weekend came bright and clear, the air cool but the sky a brilliant blue. Hazel's heart danced as she tightened Spartan's girth. Today wasn't a lesson day, or a group trail with friends. Today was just her and Narni, riding side by side.

Narni clipped Biccy's reins and swung into the saddle with practiced ease. Hazel loved the way her grandmother always looked so comfortable on a horse.

"Ready, love?" Narni called, her smile crinkling the corners of her eyes.

"Ready!" Hazel answered, settling into Spartan's saddle.

They set off at a walk, hooves crunching the gravel driveway before softening to muffled thuds on the bush track. Gum trees arched overhead, their leaves whispering in the breeze. Birds flitted from branch to branch, wallabies rustling in the undergrowth.

Hazel breathed deeply, letting the fresh morning air fill her chest. "I can't believe Biccy's here," she said, glancing at the golden mare moving steadily beside Spartan.

"She's enjoying herself already," Narni said, patting Biccy's neck. "And I think she likes Spartan's company."

The two horses walked in harmony, Biccy's golden coat gleaming in the sunlight, Spartan's dark mane rippling like silk. Hazel felt her shoulders relax, a happy warmth spreading through her.

After a while, they followed a track that dipped between two ridges. The ground was damp from last week's rain, and little streams trickled alongside them. Spartan flicked an ear forward, and Hazel spotted the reason why.

"Look, Narni!"

Just ahead, an echidna waddled across the track, spines bristling as it snuffled through the leaves. Spartan halted, ears pricked, but calm. Biccy lowered her head curiously, watching the spiny creature trundle out of sight.

Hazel giggled. "I've never seen one up this close on a ride before!"

"Nature always has surprises for us," Narni said softly. "That's one of the joys of trail riding, you never know what you'll see."

They carried on, winding deeper into the bush until the trees opened to a clearing where a narrow river crossed their path. The horses lowered their heads for a closer look, nostrils flaring as they sniffed the water. Spartan pawed at the shallows, sending a playful splash across the surface. Hazel nudged his sides, urging him forward, and with a great stomp he waded through, sending cool water spraying up over her boots and legs.

Hazel shrieked and laughed, water dripping down her jeans, while Narni chuckled as Biccy stepped calmly after them. Hazel grinned from ear to ear. "That was so much fun!" she called back.

On the far side of the river, the land opened into a wide field scattered with wildflowers, their colours swaying in the breeze. Hazel's eyes sparkled at the sight. What a perfect place.

"Shall we stop for lunch?" Narni asked, sliding from Biccy's saddle.

Hazel nodded eagerly, swinging down from Spartan's back. They loosened the girths and let the horses graze while they spread a blanket under a shady gum. From Narni's saddlebag came sandwiches, apples, and a thermos of tea.

Hazel bit into her sandwich, looking around at the wildflowers. "This is the best day," she said between bites. "Riding with you, spotting the echidna, splashing in the river, having a picnic… it feels like an adventure."

Narni smiled, pouring tea into a cup. "It is an adventure. And I think you're ready for many more." Her eyes twinkled. "Especially when you have your own horse one day."

Hazel hugged her knees, grinning at the thought. "I can't wait, Narni. I just know my horse is out there somewhere."

They sat together, eating and laughing, while the horses grazed nearby. Spartan lifted his head once, dark eyes watching Hazel, and Biccy flicked her tail against a fly. The sun warmed their backs, and for a little while, everything felt perfect.

Hazel leaned against Narni's shoulder with a happy sigh. She'd remember this day forever, not just the ride, but the feeling of being exactly where she belonged.

They tightened their girths and mounted again, ready for the trek home. Hazel turned to Narni with a cheeky grin. "Race you to the river!" she called.

Before Narni could answer, Hazel gave Spartan a nudge and they bounded down the small hill, Hazel's laughter ringing out with the sound of Narni chuckling behind her. Spartan's strides carried them swiftly to the water's edge, and Hazel whooped with delight as they splashed straight into the shallows.

She guided him downstream, letting him paw and stomp, sending arcs of cool water flying. Hazel squealed and leaned forward, hugging his neck as the spray hit her boots. "Good boy, Spartan! Look at you go!"

Narni followed on Biccy, shaking her head fondly as she watched the pair playing in the water. "All right, you two troublemakers," she laughed. "Come on now, or you'll end up soaked through and freezing before we're home!"

The afternoon light dappled through the gum trees, and the horses, bellies full of grass from their grazing, walked with lazy contentment. Hazel and Narni chatted softly about the flowers they'd seen, the birds that had sung overhead, and of course, Hazel's dream of her own horse.

When they reached the barn, Hazel pulled Spartan to a halt, blinking in surprise. By the stable doors, someone was brushing Marble's glossy chestnut coat.

"Aunt Becky!" Hazel exclaimed.

Becky looked up, her arm wrapped in a smaller cast now, neat and white against her jumper. She smiled sheepishly. "Caught me, didn't you?"

Hazel swung down from Spartan, rushing over. "But… should you really be here? You're supposed to be resting!"

Becky gave a half shrug, careful of her arm. "Probably not," she admitted. "But how can I stay away? The barn feels like home, and Marble needs the attention. Besides, I can still hold a brush in my good hand."

Hazel shook her head, though she couldn't help smiling. "You're as bad as me, Aunt Becky."

"Runs in the family," Narni teased, sliding down from Biccy.

The three of them laughed together as Spartan and Biccy blew warm breaths toward Marble, the horses greeting each other like old friends. For Hazel, the moment glowed bright; her grandmother, her aunt, and the horses, all together in the place she loved most.

And in her heart, the dream of her very own horse burned brighter than ever.

# Chapter 15

Hazel slipped Spartan's bridle off and hung it carefully on its hook, the smell of oiled leather warm in the air. Spartan shook his mane, sending strands of black hair flying, before lowering his head to snatch some hay from his net Hazel had tied. Biccy chewed contentedly in the next stall, her golden coat glowing in the afternoon light.

Narni leaned against the stable door, smiling as she watched Hazel brush Spartan down. "You've gotten quick with those hands. I remember when you needed two tries to even lift a saddle."

Hazel laughed. "I still nearly drop it sometimes! But Spartan's so patient with me."

From across the yard came the steady rhythm of brushing. Becky, one-handed but stubborn, was tending to Marble again. Hazel frowned, stepping over. "Aunt Becky, are you

sure you should be doing that much? You only just got that smaller cast."

Becky gave a guilty grin, stroking Marble's glossy shoulder with her free hand. "You're right, I probably shouldn't but, I miss everyone, and Marble looks forward to this as much as I do."

Hazel shook her head but smiled. "You'll never change."

Before Becky could reply, the crunch of tyres on gravel made all three turn. A white Ute pulled into the yard, a horse trailer hitched behind it. The logo on the side read *Riverbend Equine Vets*.

"Oh," Narni murmured, straightening. "Looks like someone's called the vet."

Hazel's curiosity prickled as the vet, a tall woman in a navy jacket, climbed out with a medical bag. A group of older riders were gathered near Opal's stall, their worried voices carrying across the barn.

"Come on," Becky said softly, leading the way.

They found Opal standing quietly, her black coat still glossy but her usual sparkle dulled. She flicked her ears as the vet ran a practiced hand down her neck, then pressed a stethoscope gently against her flank. Izzy, Opal's new owner, chewed her lip anxiously.

"She just hasn't been herself," Izzy explained. "Not eating properly, a bit lazy in her work. It's so unlike her."

The vet frowned thoughtfully, then said, "I think the best step is to scan her. That'll tell us what's going on."

Hazel and her friends crowded by the fence, wide-eyed, as the vet set up a portable ultrasound unit. Opal stood quietly as the cold gel was applied, her ears flicking but her body calm. The screen flickered, and the vet moved the probe carefully into place.

"There we go…" the vet murmured, adjusting the angle. Then she smiled. "Well, that explains it."

Izzy leaned forward nervously. "What? What is it?"

The vet turned the screen slightly so Izzy could see. "Opal is in foal. And not just newly in foal either, she's quite a way along."

The group gasped. Hazel's heart leapt into her throat. A foal!

"In foal?" Izzy repeated, her face a mix of shock and disbelief. "But she was supposed to be my new show prospect! I never expected—"

"It happens more often than people realise," the vet said gently. "Especially if mares run in larger herds. The important thing is she seems healthy, and the foal looks well too. You'll need to adjust her workload, though."

Izzy swallowed. "What can I still do with her?"

"Don't stop everything cold turkey," the vet explained. "She's been working up until now, so light riding is fine for the next few months—walk, trot, some gentle schooling. But no hard training, no big spins or sliding stops. Then, as she gets closer to foaling, drop her work down to groundwork only, hand-walking, lunging, just enough to keep her moving."

Izzy nodded slowly, still processing. "So, she can stay fit, but no pressure."

"Exactly," the vet confirmed. "And you'll need to prepare a safe paddock for her when the foal arrives."

Opal sighed softly, leaning into Izzy's hand as if she understood. Izzy's eyes softened, though her shoulders sagged. "I thought she'd be my competition horse this season," she whispered. "But now… I guess her story's changing."

Narni gave a wise smile. "That's horses for you. They always keep us guessing. Sometimes the best surprises come when we least expect them."

Hazel couldn't tear her eyes from Opal. Just days ago, she had dazzled the whole yard with her reining moves. Now, the thought of a foal growing inside her made her seem even more magical, like she was carrying a secret gift. Hazel's own dream of a horse shimmered even brighter.

Becky, still brushing Marble with her good hand, caught Hazel's expression and smiled

knowingly. "Still dreaming of your own horse, Hazel?"

Hazel nodded firmly. "More than ever. I know it means hard work and looking after them rain hail or shine no matter what but, I am ready for all of it"

Becky winked. "The right horse is out there waiting, I'm sure."

# Chapter 16

The news about Opal being in foal spread through the yard like wildfire. Everywhere Hazel went, riders were whispering about the foal-to-be, their voices full of excitement and curiosity. But Izzy still looked lost, her brow furrowed whenever she glanced at Opal.

One afternoon, Hazel found Becky standing by Marble's stall, her arm still wrapped in its smaller cast, watching the young chestnut graze in his paddock. Izzy was nearby, Opal's reins loose in her hands.

"It still feels strange," Izzy admitted, stroking Opal's neck. "I bought her to be my reining horse, and now she's going to be a mum instead. I don't know what to do with myself this season."

Becky tilted her head, thoughtful. "Well," she said slowly, "I might have an idea. It's a bit unorthodox, but hear me out."

Izzy looked up, curious.

"Marble's only three," Becky continued, "but reining was always what I intended for him. I've started him lightly, nothing too heavy yet. With me laid up for a while, I can't give him the consistent work he needs. You're an experienced rider, and you've got the time and the hunger to show. What if we worked out a plan for you to bring him on this season?"

Izzy blinked, surprised. "You'd… let me ride Marble?"

Becky nodded. "On one condition— everything's done slowly and fairly. He's still young, so no rushing. We build him up carefully, with lots of guidance, and I'll be here to oversee things even if I can't ride myself. You'd have to accept he's green and still learning, but he's smart and willing. He could shine in the right hands."

Izzy's eyes lit up. "Becky, I don't know what to say… that would be amazing." She looked down at Marble, who tossed his head as if he knew he was being discussed. "He's beautiful—and he's got that spark. I'd love to work with him."

Hazel, listening from the fence, felt her heart swell. She remembered how wild Marble had looked on the trail when Grace spooked him, and how steady he had become walking beside Spartan. It made her proud to think he might now step into a new role.

"So, we'll make a plan," Becky said firmly. "Light work to start—lots of groundwork, balance, and trust-building. Then short rides, nothing too much for his body yet. By the time the seasons in full swing, you'll know whether he's ready to show. And even if he's not, the training will set him up for the future."

Izzy grinned, her shoulders finally relaxing. "Thank you, Becky. Truly. This gives me hope for the season."

Becky smiled, brushing Marble's mane gently with her good hand. "And it helps me too. I hate sitting still while I heal. At least this way, I'll still be part of the work."

Narni, who had been listening quietly, chuckled. "Sounds like a win-win to me. Opal gets her time to be a mum, Marble gets his start, and you both get what you need."

Hazel couldn't help grinning. "And Marble gets to show everyone how clever he is." She leaned over the fence, rubbing the chestnut's soft nose. "Good boy, Marble. You've got a big job now."

Marble snorted, his ears flicking forward as if he agreed.

For Hazel, it was another reminder of what her parents kept telling her horses come with surprises, challenges, and changes. But with patience, teamwork, and love, everything could fall into place.

# Chapter 17

Saturday morning the arena was buzzing. The riders gathered at the mounting block, their voices overlapping in bursts of chatter.

"Did you hear?" Sophie whispered as she tightened her girth. "Opal's in foal! There's going to be a foal in the yard!"

Ella giggled, eyes wide. "I still can't believe it. She looked so sleek and strong in the arena, and now she's going to be a mum."

Oliver, perched on his chestnut pony, puffed out his chest. "I bet it's going to be the most beautiful foal ever. I hope it has four white socks like her."

Huxley rolled his eyes good-naturedly as Suki tugged at the reins, trying to eat grass. "I just hope it's better behaved than this one."

Hazel swung into Spartan's saddle, her heart racing with the buzz of it all. She had never been around a foal before, only Marble, but he was nearly a yearling when Aunt Becky brought him home. The idea of one being

born right here at her yard made her stomach flutter with excitement.

"Keep your chatter short, riders," Miss Laura called, clipboard tucked under her arm as she walked to the centre of the arena. "We've work to do today."

The group urged their horses into walk, circling around the arena's edge. Spartan's steady stride made Hazel feel taller in the saddle, as though nothing could go wrong with him beneath her.

Miss Laura raised her voice. "Today we'll practice transitions—walk to trot, trot to halt, then into canter if you're ready. Smooth, controlled, and only when I give the signal. Understood?"

A chorus of "Yes, Miss Laura!" rang out.

The first few transitions went well, Oliver's chestnut stepped brightly into trot, Sophie's pony halted neatly, Ella's pony tried to sneak a nibble of grass but was quickly corrected. Hazel gave Spartan the softest nudge, and he flowed into trot as though he had read her mind. She couldn't help grinning.

Then Grace entered the arena, Maverick gleaming as usual, his tail plaited, and his coat polished to perfection. She slid into line with the others, nose tilted high.

"Some of us don't need to practice transitions," she said under her breath as she passed Hazel. "Maverick's already perfect."

Hazel bit her lip, refusing to rise to it. She focused on Spartan instead, giving his neck a proud pat. *Perfect isn't everything. Connection matters too.*

Miss Laura clapped her hands. "Good. Now let's move into 20 metre circles."

Hazel guided Spartan carefully into a circle, her hands soft but steady. Across the arena, Huxley urged Suki into a wobbly circle of his own, laughing as the little mare tried to cut corners.

"You can do better than that, Suki," he joked, steering her back on track.

"Lovely work, Hazel!" Miss Laura called. "Spartan's listening beautifully today."

Hazel's cheeks glowed as she continued to focus on the exercise.

From the other side of the arena, Grace narrowed her eyes, her expression sharp as a tack. Maverick moved smoothly beneath her, but her smile was tight, her jaw clenched.

"Change the rein!" Miss Laura instructed.

The group steered across the diagonal, hooves drumming in a neat rhythm—well, mostly neat. Ella's pony zigzagged, Suki broke into an unasked-for canter, and Oliver's chestnut snorted happily through the whole thing. Hazel guided Spartan straight and true, his stride long and powerful.

By the time Miss Laura called for a walk break, the riders were flushed and laughing, the ponies blowing softly.

Hazel stroked Spartan's mane, her heart light. The lesson had been hard work, but she felt proud of how far she'd come.

As they circled down to the far end to cool off, Sophie leaned over with a grin. "Hazel, when Opal's foal comes, you'll have to help look after it. You're so good with the young ones already."

Hazel's stomach fluttered at the thought. A foal right here, in the yard and maybe soon, her very own horse too.

She smiled, her eyes bright with longing. "I'd love that."

When the lesson finished, the children untacked their ponies and settled them with hay. But instead of rushing off, they lingered by the arena fence. There was more to see today, Izzy was bringing Marble out for his very first reining session.

Hazel leaned forward eagerly as Izzy led the chestnut into the arena. His white blaze caught the sunlight, his muscles taut with energy. "Come on, Marble," Hazel whispered. "Show them what you can do."

Becky stood just inside the gate, her cast resting in a sling, giving quiet instructions. "Start with groundwork, keep him soft and listening."

Izzy worked Marble on the long line first. He jogged in a wide circle, ears flicking toward

Becky's voice. After a few laps, Becky nodded. "Good. Now up you get, but don't ask for too much. Just let him move."

Izzy swung lightly into the saddle. Marble pranced at first, unsure, but with steady guidance he settled into a jog, his head dropping into a round frame. Hazel felt her chest swell with pride.

"Look at him!" Oliver said. "He's like a different horse from the trail."

"He's smart," Huxley added. "You can see he's thinking."

Ella clasped her hands together. "And he's so pretty."

Grace, perched on Maverick just outside the arena, gave a cold laugh. "Pretty doesn't win shows. He's green as grass. He'll never be competition for real reining horses, especially not this season."

Hazel bristled, but before she could reply Sophie said firmly, "Every horse starts green, Grace. Even Maverick had to learn once."

Grace rolled her eyes, turning Maverick away with a flick of her reins.

Inside the arena, Izzy guided Marble through gentle circles and a few careful changes of direction. He snorted, stretching into the contact, and for a moment, Hazel caught a glimpse of what Becky had always seen in him—a spark of brilliance waiting to grow.

"Good boy," Izzy praised, patting his neck.

Hazel's heart fluttered. Marble wasn't just the nervous youngster who had spooked on the trail anymore. He was beginning his journey, just like Hazel dreamed of beginning hers with her very own horse.

As her dad's car pulled into the drive to collect her, Hazel tore her eyes from the arena. She couldn't wait to tell him all about her day.

# Chapter 18

A month slipped by, and the yard had settled into a new rhythm. Opal's belly was beginning to show the tiniest roundness, and everyone still whispered about the foal that would one day gallop across the paddocks. Hazel never tired of daydreaming about it, what colour would it be? Would it have Opal's star and socks?

But it wasn't just Opal who had changed, Marble had too.

Hazel leaned on the arena fence, her chin resting on folded arms, as Izzy guided Marble through a neat lope circle. His chestnut coat gleamed, and his strides looked more balanced now, more controlled. The nervous energy he had carried that first lesson was gone, replaced by a growing confidence.

"Good boy, Marble," Izzy praised, her voice steady. "Now sit back—aaaand stop."

Marble slid neatly to a halt, sand spraying under his hooves. It wasn't as long or dramatic as Opal's stops had been, but it was smooth and straight. Becky, standing nearby with her arm still in its cast sling, clapped one hand against her thigh.

"That's it! He's starting to get it."

Hazel's heart swelled with pride. Marble was really becoming a reining horse—just as Becky had always believed he could.

"Wow," Oliver said, wide-eyed beside her. "That was almost like a proper sliding stop!"

"He's so much better," Sophie agreed. "I didn't think a month would make such a difference."

Huxley nodded, patting Suki who was tied at the fence, watching. "Shows what good training does."

Grace, perched high on Maverick nearby, snorted. "Please. That wasn't a real stop. Maverick could do ten times better in his sleep. Marble will never catch up to horses like him."

Hazel felt her cheeks burn, but before she could reply, Becky spoke from the centre of

the arena. "Every horse learns at their own pace, Grace. Maverick's had years of training with top riders. Marble's had four weeks. Don't compare apples to oranges."

Grace's mouth snapped shut, her cheeks flushed red.

Hazel hid a small smile. Becky always knew just what to say.

Marble jogged a victory circle, ears flicked happily forward, as if he knew he had impressed everyone—everyone who mattered, anyway.

Hazel whispered under her breath, "Good boy, Marble. You'll show her one day."

As Izzy cooled him out, Becky came over to the group at the fence. "He's got a long way to go, but he's coming along better than I hoped. With steady work, he'll be ready to show in a few months."

Hazel's eyes sparkled. "That's amazing, Aunt Becky. I can't believe how far he's come already."

"Neither can I," Becky admitted with a smile. "But it shows what happens when a rider and horse start to understand each other. That bond—that trust—is what makes all the difference."

Hazel stroked Spartan's mane, who was standing quietly behind her. The words echoed in her chest. *Bond and trust.* That was what she wanted most of all with her very own horse.

# Chapter 19

The yard was full of chatter the next Saturday. Horses shuffled on the gravel, ponies tossed their heads, and riders bustled about tightening girths and adjusting stirrups. But today felt different — special.

Narni was there, not just as Hazel's grandmother, but standing in the middle of the arena beside Miss Laura with a clipboard in hand. Her hat shaded her eyes, and Biccy dozed behind the rails, golden and calm.

Hazel could hardly believe it. "Narni, are you really teaching us today?" she whispered, giving Spartan's nose a quick kiss before mounting.

"Just for today," Narni said with a wink. "I'm heading home soon with Biccy, but I thought I'd leave you all with something new to think about."

Miss Laura clapped her hands. "All right, everyone, today's lesson is going to be a bit different. Narni's joining us to run a Western trail class. You'll get to try some obstacles and even learn the start of a reining movement. Don't worry, we'll take it step by step."

The riders exchanged excited looks. Oliver's eyes gleamed, Sophie bounced in her saddle, and Huxley gave Suki a reassuring pat, though the little mare already looked like she was plotting mischief.

Narni started off by demonstrating each obstacle, showing the riders exactly what they needed to do. Hazel leaned on the fence, eyes wide, as Biccy stepped neatly over the bridge, bent gracefully around the poles, and halted perfectly in the box. There was such calm confidence in the way Narni rode, quiet hands, steady seat, gentle words. Hazel couldn't help but smile. She loved watching Narni do her thing with Biccy. To Hazel, it was like watching magic.

The first obstacle was easy, walk over a wooden bridge. Spartan's hooves thudded across with steady confidence, and Hazel sat tall, smiling as Miss Laura called, "Lovely, Hazel!" Suki, of course, tried to leap it in one

bound, earning a laugh from the group, and Oliver's chestnut hesitated before sniffing the boards and walking on.

Next came the bending poles. Hazel guided Spartan carefully between them, using her legs to steer, just as Narni had taught her. "Nice use of your legs," Narni called encouragingly. "That's what makes a horse soft and willing."

Finally, Narni motioned to a square of four poles laid out on the ground. "Here's the new bit," she said, her voice carrying across the arena. "In reining, one of the hardest moves is the spin. Today, you're going to try the very first step, turning one full, slow circle inside this square. No rushing — it's about balance and control."

Hazel's eyes widened. A spin! She'd seen Marble practice them with Izzy and Becky, and they looked thrilling. Now it was her turn to try, even if only the very beginning.

One by one, the riders entered the square. Oliver's chestnut fumbled the turn, stepping over a pole, but Miss Laura praised his effort. "That's why we practice — good try!" Ella's pony managed a neat half-spin before stalling. Huxley laughed as Suki spun too fast, then darted out of the square.

Then it was Hazel's turn. She guided Spartan into the square, her hands soft on the reins. "Easy, boy," she whispered. "Just follow me."

She turned her body gently, adding light pressure with her leg. Spartan shifted, stepped, then pivoted smoothly, his hind feet anchoring while his front end traced the circle. Hazel's heart soared. It wasn't fast or fancy, but it was a spin — their first spin!

"Yes, Hazel!" Narni called, clapping. "That's exactly how it starts. One good step at a time."

Hazel grinned so wide her cheeks hurt. Spartan flicked an ear back as if to say, *See? We can do this too.*

When everyone had tried, Miss Laura and Narni lined them up. "Well done," Miss Laura said. "That was a lot of new skills today. Remember, trail classes aren't just about obstacles, they're about trust and communication."

"And patience," Narni added with a wink. "You don't need to be the fastest or the flashiest. What matters is the bond you're building."

Grace, who had been sitting stiffly on Maverick through the whole thing, muttered, "Well, some of us already have that bond." But Hazel ignored her. Today wasn't about Grace.

As the lesson ended, Hazel dismounted, her cheeks still glowing. She hugged Spartan's neck. "We did it, boy. Our very first spin."

She looked over to Narni, who was stroking Biccy's golden mane. Hazel's heart squeezed. Soon Biccy would be going home, and Narni too. But this lesson — this memory — she'd keep forever.

As the other riders were leading their ponies to the rail, Narni called out, "Huxley, bring Suki over here a moment."

Huxley looked a little nervous as he guided the spotted mare across. "She wasn't very good, was she? She just bolted out of the square."

Narni chuckled, her eyes twinkling. "Oh, she was cheeky, no doubt about that. But did you feel what she did before she darted? That quick little turn around?"

Huxley frowned, thinking back. "Yeah… she spun really fast for a second."

"Exactly," Narni said warmly. "That was a natural spin. She's got the instinct for it. With some training, Suki might be very well suited to reining. She's quick on her feet and sharp in the brain. That's half the battle."

Huxley's eyes widened. "Really? You think she could be good at it?"

"I don't just think," Narni said with a smile, patting Suki's neck. "I know. She surprised me today. And sometimes the cheeky ones are the best, they just need to learn to use their mischief in the right way."

Hazel grinned at Huxley. "See? She wasn't being bad. She was showing off!"

Huxley laughed, a big smile on his face. "Guess she just wanted to prove she's special too." He gave Suki an affectionate scratch between the ears.

As they all left the arena together, Hazel's heart felt full, for herself, for Spartan, and now for Huxley and Suki too. Narni's words had lit a spark in both of them.

From behind them came a sharp laugh. Grace had dismounted Maverick and was walking with another girl from the older riders, her polished boots crunching on the gravel. She leaned in and muttered just loud enough for Hazel and Huxley to hear, "As if that little spotted thing is good for anything."

Hazel's cheeks burned, but before she could reply, Huxley squared his shoulders and gave Suki a gentle pat. "She's good enough for me," he said quietly, his voice steady.

Suki snorted as though agreeing, flicking her tail in Maverick's direction. Hazel stifled a grin. Grace could sneer all she wanted, Suki didn't need her approval. Neither did Huxley.

Narni, walking just ahead, had clearly caught the remark too. She glanced over her shoulder, her eyes sharp but calm. "Sometimes the smallest horses have the biggest hearts," she said firmly, letting the words hang in the air.

Grace turned her head away with a huff, but the sting was plain on her face.

Hazel met Huxley's eye, and both of them smiled. They didn't need Grace to believe in Suki they had Narni, each other, and the truth of what they had seen in the arena today.

# Chapter 20

The morning was cool and grey when Hazel arrived at the yard. The horse trailer was already backed up to the barn, and Biccy stood tied beside it, her golden coat gleaming even under the dull sky. Narni was brushing her mane, the strokes slow and tender.

Hazel's heart sank. "So it's really time?" she asked softly, running her hand down Spartan's reins.

Narni looked up and gave a warm smile. "Yes, love. I sadly have to go back to work and Biccy needs some rest. She's not young anymore. But I'll be back in a few weeks for another visit. Even if it's without Biccy, I'll still be here for you."

Hazel hugged her tightly. "I'll miss you both so much."

"We'll miss you too," Narni said, leaning in for a hug. "But you won't be short of horses to keep you busy. You've got Spartan, Marble—

and I'd say you'll be on foal watch in a couple of months as well."

Hazel pressed her face against Biccy's warm neck, breathing in her sweet grassy scent one last time. "Goodbye, girl. Thank you for the ride. You were perfect." Biccy flicked her ears and nudged Hazel's shoulder as though she understood.

Together, Narni and Hazel led her up the ramp. Biccy stepped into the trailer without fuss, her tail swishing softly as Narni secured the partitions. Hazel's throat tightened as the door swung shut.

"I'll be back soon," Narni promised, giving Hazel's braid a playful tug. "And by then, maybe there'll be more talk of your horse, hmm?"

Hazel's heart fluttered. She hoped so.

Later that afternoon, Hazel found Becky by the tack room, her arm finally free of its cast. She was flexing her fingers gingerly, wincing a little but grinning all the same.

"It feels strange," Becky admitted, rolling her wrist. "Weak, but free at last."

Hazel's face lit up. "So does that mean you can ride again soon?"

"Not quite yet," Becky said with a laugh. "I need to build my strength back first. But I'll be back in the saddle before too long. And it means I can help with Marble properly again. Poor boy's been wondering why his mum's been standing on the sidelines."

Hazel looked over to Marble, grazing peacefully in the paddock. "He's doing so well with Izzy, Aunt Becky. You must be proud."

"I sure am," Becky said warmly. She put her good hand on Hazel's shoulder. "And I'm proud of you, too. You've stepped up in ways I never expected. You're proving you're ready for more."

Hazel's chest swelled at her aunt's words. She glanced at Spartan, who nickered softly from his stall, and at Marble, who flicked his tail in the paddock. The yard felt a little emptier without Biccy, but with Aunt Becky recovering and Narni's promise to return, Hazel's world still felt full of hope.

# Chapter 21

The barn felt quieter without Narni and Biccy. Hazel noticed it the moment she arrived for her Saturday lesson, the golden mare's stall was empty, and the space seemed bigger somehow, as if it missed her presence too.

Hazel gave Spartan a pat as she tied up his hay net. "It feels strange without Biccy here," she whispered. He flicked an ear back at her, then lowered his head to for a scratch, as if to say *I'm still here*. Hazel smiled softly.

Out in the arena, the buzz of the lesson was building. Oliver was already warming up his chestnut, calling across the ring to Sophie and Ella, who were giggling as their ponies' snorted clouds of steam into the crisp morning air. Huxley was trotting Suki in a small circle, her spotted rump swinging playfully as though she couldn't decide whether to behave or not.

"Morning, Hazel!" Oliver waved, his grin wide.

"Morning!" she called back, swinging into Spartan's saddle. The familiar creak of leather and Spartan's steady warmth under her made the barn feel like home again, even without Biccy.

Miss Laura clapped her hands. "Right, riders! Today we're back to basics, accuracy, rhythm, and control. Remember, smooth transitions are the foundation for everything else."

As the group moved off at a walk, Grace guided Maverick into the arena, his silver-grey coat glistening like polished stone. She sat tall, her chin tipped slightly higher than everyone else's.

"Honestly," Hazel heard her mutter to one of the older girls, "it's about time we did something more advanced. Maverick's getting bored."

Hazel bit her lip but said nothing. Instead, she focused on Spartan, feeling his steady stride beneath her. Grace could boast all she liked, Hazel knew that every lesson, even the simple ones, made her a better rider.

"Hazel, lovely position," Miss Laura called. "Keep that contact soft and ask for trot when you're ready."

Hazel gave a gentle squeeze, and Spartan lifted into a smooth trot. She grinned, letting the rhythm carry her around the arena. Out of the corner of her eye, she saw Huxley urging Suki forward. The little mare gave a cheeky buck, earning a chorus of giggles from the watching riders.

"Control, Huxley!" Miss Laura reminded, though her smile showed she wasn't too cross.

As the lesson went on, Hazel felt her confidence grow. Even without Narni at the fence, she could hear her grandmother's words in her head: *Bond and trust. That's what makes the difference.*

When they lined up at the end for cool-down, Sophie leaned over. "Did you hear? Becky's almost ready to ride again. Maybe she'll be able to get back on Marble!"

Hazel's heart leapt. "Really? That's amazing, I haven't caught up with her since last weekend."

"And Izzy says Marble's improving every day," Ella added.

Hazel's eyes sparkled at the thought. *I wonder if Izzy will ride Marble today,* she mused, giving Spartan's mane an affectionate stroke.

Just then, Aunt Becky stepped out of the barn, her smile wide as she headed toward the arena rail. "Morning, Hazel!" she called. "I'm going to steal Spartan now your lesson's finished, before he cools down too much." Her eyes twinkled mischievously. "I thought I might take my first ride back on him instead of Marble. He's the safe option for a wobbly old arm!" She laughed, and Spartan flicked an ear as if he agreed.

Hazel lingered by the rail, her hands resting on the smooth wood as Aunt Becky swung gracefully into Spartan's saddle. Even with her arm still a little stiff, Becky sat tall and balanced, her seat light but secure. Spartan moved forward at her cue, his black mane rippling as he circled the arena.

Hazel loved watching them together. Becky's cues were so subtle, almost invisible, but Spartan seemed to understand every shift of her weight. They trotted neat circles, then lengthened into a steady canter. Hazel sighed with contentment. Spartan looked magnificent under Becky, powerful yet kind.

The sound of hooves behind made Hazel glance back. Izzy was leading Marble into the arena, the young chestnut gleaming after weeks of careful work. "Mind if I join you?" she called.

"Of course not," Becky replied warmly, slowing Spartan to a jog. "Let's see what the boy's got today."

Hazel's eyes brightened. She leaned forward eagerly as Izzy swung into the saddle. Marble stepped out confidently, his strides more balanced and rhythmic than Hazel remembered. Becky guided Spartan to one side of the arena while Izzy asked Marble for a small circle, then another, before pushing

him into a lope. His ears flicked back attentively, waiting for her next cue.

"Good, Izzy!" Becky called encouragingly. "Now ask for a stop."

Marble sat deep into his hindquarters and slid a short but tidy stop, sand spraying from under his hooves. Hazel's jaw dropped. In just six weeks, Marble had learned more than she imagined possible.

Becky gave a low whistle. "Not bad at all. He's catching on fast."

For the next few minutes, they rode side by side, Becky guiding Spartan through neat but simple circles, while Izzy tested Marble on spins and small sliding stops. Hazel's eyes flicked between them, Spartan's steady, basic movements and Marble's flashy new reining tricks. Spartan was beautiful and dependable, but Marble's progress dazzled everyone watching.

Hazel's chest tightened. She didn't love Spartan any less, in fact, she felt even more grateful for him. But as Marble spun neatly pivoting on the spot, Hazel couldn't help thinking: *One day, I want a horse I can bring along like that. From the start. It would be so rewarding.*

# Chapter 22

A month rolled by in a blur of lessons, schooling, and evening rides. The air was warmer now, the paddocks thick with green grass, Opal was getting rounder, and the buzz of the approaching reining season seemed to hum through the whole yard.

Only two weeks remained before the first show. Marble and Izzy had been training almost daily, each session sharper than the last. Hazel often found herself leaning over the arena rail, wide-eyed, as Marble spun neatly on his hindquarters or slid to a smooth stop, sand spraying under his hooves. He looked every inch the reining prospect Becky had promised he could be.

But Hazel hadn't just been watching. Izzy had taken her under her wing in small ways, offering friendly tips whenever she could. "Keep your hands soft, Hazel—Spartan likes it better that way," she'd say, or "Ask for that turn with your leg first, then guide with the rein." Slowly, Hazel began to experiment with

Spartan, trying tiny circles, careful stops, even getting some slow spins.

Aunt Becky rode Spartan, too, her arm now fully healed and her grin as wide as ever. Sometimes she and Hazel shared the big black horse in a session, swapping over so each could try the same pattern. Spartan wasn't as sharp or flashy as Marble, but he was willing, steady, and eager to please. Hazel loved the feel of him listening, learning with her.

One afternoon, as the sun dipped low and the yard turned golden, Becky and Izzy sat side by side on the arena rail, watching Hazel guide Spartan through a careful circle. His ears flicked back to her, his stride steady and responsive. When Hazel sat deep and gave the cue, Spartan shifted his weight, stopping sharply with his hindquarters tucked neatly beneath him. It wasn't the long, dramatic slide of a seasoned Reiner, but it was close— close enough to make Becky and Izzy exchange a quick, knowing glance. Hazel leaned forward, patting Spartan's neck with a grin that lit up her whole face.

"They are coming along," Izzy said quietly.

Becky nodded. "She's more than coming along. She might just be ready to try a class."

Izzy's eyes sparkled. "The youth beginner class at the show?"

Becky smiled slyly. "Exactly."

Hazel trotted Spartan toward them, cheeks flushed with pride. "How was that?"

"Lovely," Becky said warmly. "Spartan's listening beautifully."

Hazel beamed, unaware of the glance shared between Becky and Izzy. The two women didn't say a word more, but the decision was made, Marble and Izzy would enter the show in the green horse division and Hazel and Spartan would quietly be entered in the youth beginner class.

As Hazel cooled Spartan down, humming to herself, her heart was already racing with excitement for the show season. She didn't know it yet, but her own name would be on the entry list too.

# Chapter 23

The week before the show, the whole yard buzzed with energy. Izzy and Marble were sharper than ever, their spins crisp and their stops sliding further each day. Hazel and Spartan were also finding their rhythm, their circles smoother and their halts tidier. Every ride left Hazel glowing with pride, though she never once imagined herself in the same league as Izzy.

On Saturday morning, Hazel was finishing her breakfast when a knock came at the door. She looked up in surprise as Omie and Aunt Becky walked in, smiling in a way that made her suspicious.

"Morning, love," Omie said, giving Hazel a quick hug. "We've got plans today."

Hazel frowned. "Plans?"

Her mum stood behind them, with a knowing grin. "We thought it was time for a little outing. Come on, grab your shoes."

Still puzzled, Hazel followed them into the car. They chatted the whole way about the show season, Marble's progress, and even Opal's foal, but nobody explained what was really happening. Finally, they pulled into the car park of Hazel's favourite saddlery.

Hazel's eyes widened. "We're going shopping?"

"That's right," Omie said with a twinkle in her eye. "You'll need something special for next weekend."

Hazel blinked. "Next weekend?"

Becky just smiled and gently pushed her inside. Racks of crisp shirts, smart jackets, and neat trousers lined the walls. The smell of polished leather and new fabric filled the air.

Her mum picked out a pale blue shirt that shimmered softly in the light, holding it up under Hazel's chin. "Try this one, chook. And maybe these black show pants too and why you're at it these boots."

Hazel's stomach fluttered with excitement and nerves. She slipped into the changing room, pulled the outfit on, and stepped out to the mirror. For a moment, she hardly recognised herself. The girl looking back wasn't just Hazel in her everyday jeans and boots, she looked like a real rider, ready for the arena.

"Wow," Hazel breathed. "I look… amazing."

Behind her, Becky and Omie exchanged a secret smile.

Her mum crouched to meet Hazel's eyes in the mirror. "I'm glad you like it, Hazel, because how would you feel about wearing this in the youth beginner class next weekend?"

Hazel spun around, her eyes wide. "What?!"

Becky laughed, her voice warm with pride. "You and Spartan are entered. We wanted to surprise you. You've worked so hard, and you're ready."

For a moment, Hazel could only stare, her mouth open. Then the words sank in, and joy exploded inside her. "I'M REALLY GOING TO RIDE IN THE SHOW?!" she cried, bouncing on the spot.

Omie chuckled. "Yes, you are. And we'll all be there cheering you on." Not just us either Narni and Pop and Poppy Lils are all coming and I dare say some of your friends will want to come when they hear the news.

Hazel threw her arms around Becky, Omie, and her mum all at once. "Thank you, thank you, thank you! This is the best surprise ever!"

As she turned back to the mirror, still clutching the soft blue shirt, her cheeks glowed with excitement. Next weekend, riding Spartan, in her very first reining show.

They headed toward the checkout with Hazel's new outfit draped carefully over her arm, but when Hazel looked around, Aunt Becky had vanished.

"Where's Becky gone?" Omie asked, frowning.

Just then Becky reappeared around the corner, grinning like a cat, clutching a stunning western pad in her hands. Its colours shimmered and matched Hazel's new show shirt perfectly.

Hazel's mum and Omie raised their eyebrows in unison. "Really, Becky?"

Becky gave an exaggerated shrug. "What? Spartan needs a new pad for his collection."

They all rolled their eyes. Everyone knew Aunt Becky's saddle pad collection was already vast, but she didn't have a western pad quite this spectacular.

Becky leaned down and whispered in Hazel's ear, her voice playful. "I mean, you have to be matchy-matchy for a show."

Hazel's giggle bubbled out before she could stop it, her eyes shining. This was really happening. She wasn't just going to ride in the show, she was going to look the part too and now so was Spartan.

# Chapter 24

Before she knew it, it was the day before the show. Hazel was excited her parents had allowed her to have the day off school to help prepare the horses.

Hazel stood on a stool beside Spartan, her sleeves rolled up, suds running down her arms. Spartan gave a long, dramatic sigh as if the bath was the greatest hardship in the world.

"Oh, don't be such a baby," Hazel teased, scrubbing at a stubborn patch on his hind leg. "You'll thank me when you're the shiniest horse in the ring tomorrow."

Aunt Becky laughed as she rinsed Marble in the next wash bay. The young chestnut stamped a hoof, sending water splashing onto Becky's jeans. "See? Marble agrees with Spartan; this is all far too much effort."

Izzy grinned as she held Marble's lead rope steady. "They'll look worth it tomorrow. Just imagine the judge seeing them all polished up."

By late afternoon, the horses were spotless, the same could not be said for Hazel, Becky and Izzy. Hazel ran her hand down Spartan's gleaming coat with pride. "You look amazing, boy. We're ready."

The real work came next, packing the float. Saddle stands were folded into place, tack boxes wedged neatly, and the freshly purchased western pad Aunt Becky had surprised Hazel with went on top like a treasure. Buckets, brushes, spare gear, hay nets, everything had its spot. Hazel ticked items off the list Becky read aloud, determined not to forget a single thing.

"Clothes, hats, boots—check," Becky called. "Show numbers—check," Izzy added. "Horse cookies—check," Hazel said, grinning as she tucked Spartan's favourites into a side pocket.

As the last of the gear was stowed away, the group made their way past Opal's paddock. The sleek black mare lifted her head and wandered over, her sides rounder than ever now.

"Look at her," Izzy murmured, stroking Opal's nose. "She's really showing now."

Omie, who had come to help load hay, paused, frowning thoughtfully. "More than that… has anyone else noticed her udder?"

Hazel crouched for a closer look and gasped. "She has too! Does that mean the foal is coming soon?"

Becky exchanged a glance with Omie and Izzy. "It means she's getting closer; that's for sure. We'll have to keep an extra-close eye on her from now on, it might be time to put the foal alarm on her just in case since we don't know when her due date is"

Hazel's heart raced. A show tomorrow, and now the thought that Opal's foal could arrive in the coming weeks, it was almost too much excitement to hold.

As the sun dipped low and the horses munched happily on their evening hay, Hazel gave Spartan one last pat. "Tomorrow's the big day, big boy. Let's make it one to remember." Spartan blew softly into her hair, as if promising he'd do his best.

# Chapter 25

The alarm rang long before the sun came up. Hazel blinked sleepily, then shot upright in bed — *today was the day!* Her very first reining show.

Downstairs, the house was already alive with quiet movement. Her mum was packing sandwiches into a cooler, while her dad carried a thermos of coffee to the car. Omie slipped a packet of mints into Hazel's pocket with a wink. "For Spartan," she whispered. Poppy Lils was already in the car, ready to head to the yard. Narni and Pop would meet them at the show, it was closer to their house than to Hazel's.

By the time they reached the yard, the headlights lit up a flurry of activity. The float doors were open, hay nets already tied, and Aunt Becky was tightening the last strap on Marble's travel boots. Izzy held him steady, her expression calm but her hands fidgeting with excitement.

"Morning, team," Becky called, grinning under the glow of the floodlights. "Ready to make history?"

Hazel laughed nervously, her stomach fluttering with butterflies. She hurried to Spartan's stall, where he greeted her with a soft nicker. His mane had been neatly plaited to stop hay getting caught, and his coat still gleamed from yesterday's bath.

"You look amazing, boy," Hazel whispered, slipping him a mint. "Let's go show them what we can do."

Loading the horses was smoother than Hazel had imagined. Marble stepped into the float with only a small hesitation, and Spartan followed like the seasoned professional he was. With the ramp secured and the gear double-checked, the convoy set off toward the showgrounds.

The drive felt endless. Hazel pressed her forehead to the window, watching the stars fade into a pale dawn. Her heart thudded with every mile. *What would the arena look like? Would the other riders be older, better, braver?*

When they finally pulled in, Hazel gasped. The showgrounds stretched out before them a hive of activity, horse trailers, riders in crisp shirts, and horses gleaming like polished statues. The sound of hooves on gravel mixed with laughter, announcements over loudspeakers, and the occasional whinny.

Becky hopped out first, clapping her hands. "All right! Horses unloaded, tack checked. Let's get organised."

Hazel followed instructions as best she could, though her head swirled. She brushed Spartan's coat one more time, adjusted the shining new western pad Becky had surprised her with, and smoothed her pale blue shirt.

"You look the part, Hazel," Omie said warmly. "Like you've been doing this for years."

Hazel swallowed hard. "I don't feel like it."

Her mum knelt to straighten Hazel's collar. "It's okay to be nervous, Hazel. It doesn't matter what happens today, it's all about the experience and enjoying yourself."

As the loudspeaker crackled to life, announcing the first class of the day, Hazel's nerves turned to pure excitement. *This was it. The show had begun.*

She gave Spartan's nose a quick kiss. "Here we go, boy. Our big adventure."

Spartan flicked an ear and blew gently onto her cheek, as if to say he was ready too.

Hazel's class was the third of the day, with twelve competitors entered. Her eyes scanned the run sheet and froze. *Grace.* Really? Hazel rolled her eyes. Grace wasn't even interested in reining, she preferred dressage. But of course, she'd entered this show too.

Marble was tucked into a stall to rest until his class in the evening, so Izzy and Becky focused on helping Hazel. Together, they went over her pattern until she could almost ride it in her sleep.

When the announcer finally called the youth beginner class to the warm-up ring, Hazel's heart leapt into her throat. The group walked together toward the arena, where Narni and Pop were waiting with a big wave.

"Oh, just look at you!" Narni beamed. "You and Spartan look amazing."

Everyone wished Hazel luck before heading to their seats. Becky stayed just long enough to run through the pattern one last time, her voice steady and reassuring. Then she squeezed Hazel's hand, leaving her to the warm-up pen to wait for her name to be called.

# Chapter 26

The youth beginner class was called, and the riders filed one by one into the warm-up arena. Hazel's heart thumped as she watched Grace ahead of her, Maverick gleaming like newly fallen snow under the sunlight.

Grace's performance was, as always, tidy and precise. Maverick moved flawlessly through the pattern, his circles smooth, his transitions crisp. But there was something missing — no spark, no joy, just mechanical perfection. The judge's nod was approving, but not overly impressed.

Then Hazel's number was called.

She squeezed Spartan's reins, took a deep breath, and guided him into the ring. A cheer erupted from the sidelines, Narni and Pop waving wildly, Omie and Poppy Lils clapping, Mum and Dad calling encouragement. Even Huxley, Oliver, Sophie, and Ella had come to watch, their voices carrying over the arena fence.

Hazel's nerves melted into a smile. *We can do this, Spartan.*

The pattern began. Spartan lifted into his circles with steady confidence, Hazel sitting tall, remembering every cue Becky and Izzy had drilled into her. The crowd blurred away; it was just her and Spartan, moving together.

When she asked for the spins, Spartan turned faster than he ever had before, his shoulders light, his hind feet anchored. Hazel's grin stretched wider, they were really spinning! The crowd applauded, and Hazel felt her chest swell.

Then came the stop. She took a deep breath, asked for the lope, then sat deep, saying softly, "Whoa." Spartan slid to a sharp halt, sand spraying behind them. For a heartbeat, the arena went silent. Then the applause erupted.

Hazel patted Spartan's neck as she finished her run, her face glowing. "Good boy, you were amazing."

She guided him out of the arena, her legs shaking with exhilaration. The other riders had been strong, some much older, their horses well-schooled and polished, but Hazel didn't care. She had given her best, and Spartan had been brilliant.

When the results were announced, Hazel's stomach twisted. "In third place… Hazel and Spartan!"

Her friends cheered so loudly she thought her ears might pop. Hazel couldn't stop grinning as she trotted forward to accept her ribbon.

"In second place… Grace and Maverick."

Hazel's smile faltered slightly, but she clapped politely along with everyone else. Their scores were close, almost tied, but Hazel was proud of herself regardless.

"And in first place… Ruby Anderson on Dusty!" A tall girl Hazel didn't know beamed as she rode forward, her horse tossing his mane.

As the riders lined up to congratulate one another, Hazel's friends rushed to the rail, clapping and calling her name. "Well done, Hazel!" "Spartan was incredible!"

Hazel's cheeks glowed with pride. But as she turned to dismount, she noticed Grace sitting tall on Maverick, her ribbon limp in her hand. No one came to the rail for her. No parents, no friends, no cheers — just silence.

Hazel's heart tightened. For all Grace's perfection, she had no one to share it with. And in that moment, Hazel felt something she hadn't expected, not triumph, but a flicker of sympathy.

She stroked Spartan's mane, leaning close to whisper. "We're the lucky ones, boy. Not just because of ribbons, but because of everyone who's here for us."

Spartan flicked an ear, steady and warm, and Hazel knew she was right.

Hazel cooled Spartan off carefully, walking him until his breathing slowed and his coat dried to a healthy sheen. Back at the stalls, she set him up with fresh water, a pile of hay, and perhaps more than a few treats slipped into his feed bucket. Spartan's ears flicked

happily as he munched, his dark eyes soft and trusting. Hazel wrapped her arms around his strong neck, pressing her cheek against his silky mane.

"What a team we make," she whispered. "I'm so proud of you."

# Chapter 27

By late afternoon, the arena buzzed with anticipation. The green horse reining class was one of the biggest of the day, with nearly twenty entries, all young horses, each making their very first appearance in the show ring. There was even prize money on offer for the winners. It wasn't quite like the pro classes scheduled for later, but it was still a serious competition, and the stands were full.

Hazel could feel the excitement humming through the crowd as Izzy tightened Marble's cinch and swung into the saddle. The chestnut gelding, now sleek and muscled after months of careful training, tossed his head once before settling into the warm-up with his usual focus.

"They look amazing already," Hazel whispered, leaning against the rail.

Beside her, Becky wrung her hands, her face pale with nerves. "I know he's ready," she

said softly, almost to herself. "But oh, my word, I feel sick watching."

The announcer called for the first riders, and one after another, the young horses entered the ring. Some were steady, some rushed, and some showed flashes of brilliance. Hazel's heart pounded with every run, but she waited, saving her cheers for Izzy and Marble.

At last, their names were called. Marble trotted into the arena, ears pricked, Izzy sitting tall with calm confidence. From the first stride, Hazel knew they were different.

Their slow circles were balanced and soft, Marble moving like he was floating. Then, with the gentlest cue, he shifted into fast circles, driving forward with power and precision, before melting back into a slow, collected lope. The crowd murmured in appreciation.

"Beautiful," Narni breathed from the row behind.

Next came the rundowns. Marble surged forward in perfect straight lines, then sank deep into sliding stops, sand billowing out behind them as he tucked his hindquarters under himself. The audience gasped and clapped, and Hazel grinned so wide her cheeks hurt.

Then came the spins. Izzy set him up, and Marble turned — once, twice, three times, faster and faster, until Hazel was sure Izzy must be feeling dizzy. Yet she sat square and calm, Marble's feet a blur beneath her.

By the end of the run, the crowd was on their feet, cheering. Izzy gave Marble a grateful pat and jogged him out on a loose rein, her face glowing.

The final scores took time to calculate. Hazel and Becky sat shoulder to shoulder, holding their breath as the announcer began to call the placings.

"In third place…" Hazel leaned forward, but it wasn't Izzy's name.
"In second place…" Becky's shoulders slumped.

"They must have just missed out," Becky whispered, her eyes clouding with disappointment. "Fourth, maybe."

But then the announcer's voice boomed across the arena. "And in first place… Izzy and Marble!"

The crowd erupted. Becky gasped, her hand flying to her mouth. "They did it!"

Hazel leapt to her feet, clapping until her palms stung. Marble trotted proudly to the centre of the arena, Izzy's grin stretching from ear to ear as she accepted the blue ribbon. The young gelding's chestnut coat gleamed in the late sun, and for a moment he looked like a king.

Hazel's heart swelled. Marble had gone from a green youngster to a champion in just a few months and she had been there to see it all.

Hazel and her friends chattered excitedly as Izzy and Marble jogged out of the arena, blue ribbon pinned proudly to his bridle.

"What a performance!" Oliver said, his freckles glowing with the excitement.

"I'm in awe," Huxley added, shaking his head. "They just kept getting better and better. Every move was sharper than the last."

Sophie leaned on the rail, her eyes shining. "If that's the *green horse* class, can you imagine what the pros are going to be like?"

The group burst into laughter and applause again as Izzy trotted past, Marble flicking his ears at the cheering children like he knew exactly what he had achieved.

Together they clapped and cheered, staying glued to their seats for the last two classes of the night: the freestyle and the pro division.

The freestyles were unlike anything Hazel had ever imagined. Riders performed breathtaking runs set to music, some dressed in elaborate costumes that glittered under the arena lights. One cowboy spun his horse in a storm of dust while a violin played live from the corner of the ring. Another rider, dressed like a matador, guided her palomino through a pattern so precise Hazel forgot to breathe. Each creation was more jaw-dropping than the last.

Hazel bounced in her seat, clutching Narni's hand. "This is amazing! I didn't know reining could be like this!"

And then the pros came out. The atmosphere shifted — hushed, reverent, as if everyone knew they were about to see the best of the best. The horses were powerful, their strides long and effortless, their spins so fast the crowd gasped in unison. Sliding stops carved lines in the sand so deep they looked like tracks on a racetrack.

Hazel's eyes went wide, her heart pounding in time with the music and the crowd's applause. "One day," she whispered to herself, barely aware she'd spoken aloud. "One day, that will be me."

They packed up the float and loaded the horses, everyone moving a little slower now after such a long, exhilarating day. Aunt Becky was speaking quietly to Hazel's mum as she tightened the ramp.

"Take Hazel straight home to bed," Becky said firmly. "Izzy and I will sort the horses once we're back at the yard. She's had the biggest day, I bet she'll be asleep before you hit the highway."

Hazel hugged Narni and Pop goodbye, wrapping her arms tight around them before waving as Becky and Izzy drove off with the horses in tow.

Then she clambered into the car with her parents, Omie, and Poppy Lils. As the headlights cut through the dark, lighting the road ahead, Hazel buzzed with excitement, unable to keep still.

For the first fifteen minutes she chattered nonstop, reliving her ride step by step, re-enacting Marble's spins with her hands, dreaming up wild costume ideas for a future freestyle, and gasping all over again about the pros. "Did you see how fast they spun? And that music! And Marble, oh Marble was incredible—"

Her words tumbled out in a rush, one thought chasing another, her family smiling and nodding along.

But before long, her voice trailed away mid-sentence. The car grew quiet, the hum of the

tires steady in the night. Hazel's head lolled gently against the window; her ribbon still clutched loosely in her hand.

She was fast asleep, dreaming of horses, shows, and adventures yet to come.

# Chapter 28

Hazel blinked awake, stretching her arms wide. For a moment she couldn't work out where she was. The soft weight of her doona, the gentle ticking of the clock on her wall — *home*. She was in her own bed.

She sat bolt upright. *The show!* The memory came rushing back in a flood, Spartan's spins, Marble's blue ribbon, the costumes, the pros, the cheers. A grin spread across her face.

Hazel flung back the covers, scrambled into her jeans, and darted into the kitchen. "Morning!" she called, grabbing a piece of toast before anyone could answer. She took two big bites, then downed a glass of juice as if speed-eating would get her back to the barn faster.

Her mum chuckled from the sink. "Slow down, Hazel. The horses aren't going anywhere."

Hazel shook her head, her braid swinging. "I have to go, Mum! I need to give Spartan the biggest hug. He was *so* amazing yesterday. The best horse ever. And I want to see Marble and Izzy and everyone and—and—"

Her words tumbled over one another in a rush.

"And Opal," her dad added with a smile. "No doubt you'll want to check on her."

Hazel's eyes went wide. "Oh yes! Opal!" She shoved the last bite of toast into her mouth, grabbed her boots, and was out the door before her parents could say another word.

The morning air was crisp, carrying the scent of dew on the grass. Hazel's boots crunched on the gravel as she raced toward the barn, her heart full to bursting. She was desperate to throw her arms around Spartan's strong neck, to share every dream that had blossomed after yesterday, and to see her friends again.

And Opal — Hazel's chest fluttered with anticipation. The black mare's growing belly and new udder meant something big was coming, and Hazel didn't want to miss a single moment.

Today, after the magic of the show, the barn felt more than just her happy place. It felt like the centre of everything Hazel dreamed of becoming.

# Chapter 29

Hazel found her friends gathered by Opal's paddock, leaning on the fence while the black mare munched contentedly at the fresh grass. The morning sun lit her rounded sides, and Hazel felt her chest squeeze with anticipation.

"Morning!" Hazel called, jogging over.

"Morning!" Oliver grinned. "We were just saying, can you believe yesterday actually happened? Hazel, your stop was epic."

Hazel laughed, cheeks warming. "And Marble! I still can't believe he won."

Huxley gave a dramatic sigh. "The freestyles… I'll be thinking about those for the rest of my life."

They all burst out laughing, voices tumbling over each other as they relived every detail, the spins, the ribbons, the costumes, the pro riders who had left them speechless.

Meanwhile, Opal flicked her tail lazily and kept eating, unbothered by the chatter. Izzy crouched near her flank, gently running a hand over her belly.

"She's coming along," Izzy said. "Look here." She pointed to Opal's udder. "She's even starting to run a bit of milk. It truly can't be long now."

The group fell quiet for a moment, each of them staring at Opal in awe. The idea of a new foal made the barn feel like it was holding its breath.

Then Sophie piped up, "Let's go for a ride! Just a short one."

"Yes!" Hazel said immediately, bouncing on her toes. "Please, Izzy will you come is Aunt Becky here? Can we?"

Becky walked around the corner at the moment and chuckled, shaking her head fondly. "All right, but just a short trail to stretch the horses' legs."

Within minutes, the friends were mounted and heading down the familiar track. Marble was like a different horse, confident, ears

pricked, strides steady as if he had finally grown into himself.

"He looks amazing," Hazel said to Izzy, who nodded proudly.

The group rode together in cheerful chatter, the events of the show still sparking laughter and excitement. They walked through puddles, trotted along the sandy path, and soaked up the simple joy of being together.

By late afternoon they were back at the barn. Hazel brushed Spartan until his coat gleamed, while the others fussed over their ponies. Each horse got an extra treat, a soft pat, and murmured thanks for the ride.

When the stalls were bedded down and the last buckets filled, Hazel rested her cheek against Spartan's neck. "Goodnight, boy," she whispered. "What a weekend we've had."

The barn was quiet as the children headed home, their hearts full. Tomorrow Opal might still be waiting, or she might surprise them all.

# Chapter 30

Hazel groaned loudly as her mum called up the stairs. "Come on, Hazel, you'll miss the bus!"

"But what if Opal foals today?" Hazel called back, dragging her school jumper over her head.

"You'll find out after school," came the reply. "Now hurry up!"

Hazel stomped down the steps with her backpack, muttering to herself. The last thing she wanted was to sit through maths when there might be a foal arriving at the barn. But she had no choice. She slumped into her bus seat, hugging her lunchbox tight and counting the hours until the bell rang.

At last, when school was done, Hazel practically flew off the bus and jogged all the way to the yard. She burst through the gate, heart pounding. Opal stood quietly in her paddock, her belly round, tail swishing lazily. No foal.

Hazel sighed, shoulders slumping. "Not yet, huh, girl?"

Still, she wasn't going to waste her time. She helped sweep the aisles, refill hay nets, and top up water troughs. The steady rhythm of chores made the waiting easier. Miss Laura passed through now and then, checking tack or speaking with riders, her clipboard never far from her hand.

As the sun began to sink, the yard grew quieter. One by one, the other riders packed up and left. Miss Laura poked her head into the aisle. "Hazel, your mum just rang. She's running late from work, but will be here to collect you shortly. Do you want to wait in the office?"

Hazel shook her head. "I'll be fine."

She was the last one about, the evening air cool on her cheeks. With the yard still, she strolled toward Opal's paddock. The mare was lying down, looking like she was snoozing. Hazel leaned on the rail, watching her for a moment. Then her eyes narrowed.

Opal's breathing looked heavier. Her sides moved in short, laboured bursts. Hazel's gaze dropped lower, and her heart leapt into her throat. She could see a tiny hoof emerging.

Hazel gasped. "Oh my goodness — Opal's foaling!"

She scrambled through the gate and hurried to Opal's side, her hands shaking. "It's okay, girl. I'm here."

Then she turned and shouted with all her might. "Miss Laura! Quick, come quick!"

Laura was running before Hazel had even finished. She vaulted the rail, eyes widening as she saw the hoof. "You're right. She's foaling. Stay calm, Hazel. I'll call Izzy."

She whipped out her phone, dialling as she knelt by Opal. "Izzy! It's Laura. She's started. Yes, now. I don't know why the foaling alarm didn't go off, but she's definitely in labour. Hurry!"

Hazel knelt beside Opal's head, stroking her soft mane while Laura kept watch at the mare's hindquarters. The quiet paddock was

suddenly charged with energy, every second stretching into forever.

"Don't worry, Opal," Hazel whispered, her voice trembling with excitement and fear. "You've got this, girl. And I'm right here."

Opal was doing brilliantly, her breaths steady as each contraction rolled through her. Hazel kept whispering encouragement, stroking the mare's neck. "You're amazing, Opal. You've got this."

Thankfully, Izzy lived close by, with luck, she wouldn't miss too much of the birth.

Hazel's eyes widened as more of the foal appeared. First the tiny hooves, then a delicate little nose. She gasped, her heart leaping. "I can see the foal! Look, there is so much white!"

Miss Laura crouched nearby, calm and watchful. "That's it, Opal. One more big push, girl."

With another strong contraction, the foal slid into the world, landing safely on the grass.

Just then, tyres crunched on the gravel and a car door slammed. Running footsteps pounded across the yard. Izzy flew over the fence, breathless, just as Opal turned to nuzzle her newborn.

"Oh, Opal," Izzy cooed, her voice full of relief and joy. "You clever, clever girl."

Opal instinctively began licking her foal clean, her soft nickers filling the quiet paddock. Hazel bent closer, hardly daring to breathe. She locked eyes with the new little tyke, who blinked back at her with wide, dark eyes. Her heart felt like it might burst.

"It's a colt," Izzy announced, her voice proud and tender all at once. "And he's got all of his mother's markings… plus a huge belly splash. He's just perfect."

Hazel reached out, her fingertips brushing the colt's damp, silky coat. In that moment, she knew she would never forget the sight, Opal and her newborn, safe and sound under the soft glow of the evening sky.

Hazel's mum's car pulled into the yard just as Opal nosed at her colt's damp flank. She hurried across the grass, her eyes wide.

"Oh, Hazel — wow, just *wow!*" she exclaimed, crouching beside her daughter. "Look what you got to see. I suppose it was lucky I was running late today." She laughed, shaking her head in amazement.

They stayed together in the paddock, the cool evening wrapping around them, watching in wonder as the little colt tried to heave himself onto his long, gangly legs. He wobbled, stumbled, then found his balance, swaying unsteadily before staggering to Opal's side. With gentle nudges from his mother, he lowered his head and found his first drink of milk.

Hazel's heart soared. "He's perfect," she whispered, barely able to blink in case she missed a single moment.

But before long, her mum placed a soft hand on her shoulder. "As much as I'd love to stay and watch all night, it's time for tea and bed, Hazel. Sorry, love."

Hazel's shoulders slumped. "Do we really have to?"

Her mum smiled. "We'll come back first thing in the morning, I promise."

Izzy walked over, her face glowing, and pulled Hazel into a tight hug. "Thank you for being here for Opal, and for getting Laura to call me. I can't believe the foaling alarm failed — but you were here when Opal needed someone. I'll never forget that."

Hazel hugged her back fiercely, her eyes still fixed on the colt. Leaving was the last thing she wanted, but even as she followed her mum toward the car, she knew this day would stay etched in her memory forever.

# Chapter 31

The next morning, Hazel and her mum swung by the barn on the way to school. Hazel practically leapt from the car before it stopped rolling, racing to Opal's paddock. There he was — the little colt — curled in the long grass beside his mother, ears twitching, legs folded like stilts waiting to spring.

Izzy leaned on the rail, looking tired but glowing. "Morning, Hazel!" she laughed. "I haven't gone home yet. How could I? I didn't want to miss a thing. He's going to be such a time-waster, I can't stop watching him."

Hazel giggled, her eyes glued to the colt. "He's perfect."

Her mum checked her watch. "As much as I'd love to stay too, Hazel, we've got to get you to school."

Hazel groaned but nodded, still reluctant to leave.

"Wait a second," Izzy called, her eyes twinkling. "Hazel, since you were the very first one to meet him, how about you come up with a name?"

Hazel spun around, her mouth dropping open. "Are you *serious*?"

"Dead serious."

"Wow," Hazel breathed. "Umm… I'll have to give it some thought."

She tore herself away reluctantly, climbing back into the car. All the way to school, her mind whirled. In class, she doodled little horse heads in the margins of her worksheets, testing out names. At lunch she lay in the grass, staring at the clouds. *What name was strong enough? What name was perfect for Opal's colt?*

That afternoon, she burst through the barn doors, her backpack bouncing on her shoulders. "Hi, Spartan!" she called, slipping him a treat. She stroked his dark neck, whispering, "I'll be back soon, promise," before hurrying to Opal's paddock.

Her friends were already there, clustered at the fence, laughing as the little colt pranced around on his gangly legs, his tail sticking

straight in the air. Hazel leaned against the rail, her heart swelling.

Izzy came over, folding her arms with a smile. "So, Hazel — did you decide?"

Hazel nodded, cheeks flushed with excitement. "I think… Sampson. That's his name. What do you think?"

As if he'd heard her, the colt let out a high-pitched nicker and tossed his head before bounding in a joyful circle around Opal.

Izzy laughed. "Well, I think he agrees. Sampson it is."

The group cheered, and Hazel grinned so wide her face hurt. She had got to name Opal's foal — *Sampson!* The thought filled her with pride. She felt so privileged, as if she'd been entrusted with something truly important.

Hazel leaned on the rail a little longer, watching Sampson wobble back to his mother's side and nurse. His tiny tail twitched with every gulp, his gangly legs braced wide for balance. Hazel sighed happily. *I could waste hours just admiring him.*

But chores don't wait. With a reluctant glance back, Hazel pushed herself away from the fence. Buckets needed filling, hay nets needed topping, and stalls needed sweeping. She threw herself into the work, knowing she'd be back to check on Sampson again while she waited for her ride home.

That evening, it was her dad who pulled into the yard. Hazel ran to meet him, her face alight. "Come on! You *have* to meet Sampson!"

He laughed, following her to Opal's paddock. The colt was dozing, but at Hazel's call he gave a curious little nicker, stretching his neck.

Her dad's eyes softened as he leaned on the rail. "Well, would you look at him. Strong-looking little guy already, isn't he?"

Hazel nodded proudly. "He's perfect. Just perfect."

# Chapter 32

Over the following weeks, Sampson grew stronger by the day. His legs, once wobbly and uncertain, now carried him in joyful bursts of energy across the paddock. He bucked and kicked, tail flying like a banner, before skidding to a stop and trotting straight over to Hazel.

It became his habit, whenever Hazel appeared at the fence, Sampson would bound toward her with a cheerful nicker, pressing his soft muzzle into her hands as if she were part of his world as much as Opal was. The bond between them was clear to anyone watching.

"He really loves you," Izzy remarked one afternoon, smiling as Sampson nudged Hazel's shoulder.

Hazel beamed. "I love him too. He's the best foal in the whole world."

Between Sampson's visits, Hazel's lessons continued. With Spartan beneath her, she grew more confident each week. Her circles were rounder, her stops sharper, her cues softer. Sometimes Becky rode alongside her, sometimes Izzy offered advice, and always Hazel felt she was learning — not just to ride, but to *understand*.

And she wasn't alone. Oliver, Huxley, Sophie, and Ella had all improved too, their friendship was blossoming. They laughed through lesson games and encouraged one another over tiny jumps, and cheered when someone finally managed a tricky obstacle.

Hazel would often go home exhausted, her boots dusty and her hair full of hay, but her heart brimmed with happiness. She had Spartan, she had her friends, and was so grateful for Sampson too — a playful little foal who had already claimed a piece of her heart.

# Chapter 33

"Hazel," Izzy called one afternoon, leading Opal toward the barn. "Can I borrow you? Opal's due for her annual dentist work, and I was hoping you could keep an eye on Sampson for a bit."

Hazel's eyes lit up. "Of course!"

While the vet worked with Opal, Hazel put a little halter and lead onto Sampson's head and led him gently into the round pen. The foal's legs had grown longer, his stride bouncier, but his eyes still sparkled with mischief. Hazel unclipped the foal once they were secure in the pen, he sniffed the sand curiously, then gave a joyful buck, darting in circles around Hazel.

Hazel laughed, jogging a few steps. To her delight, Sampson followed, matching her pace. She stopped suddenly — and he stopped too, tossing his head. She skipped sideways, and he bounded after her, mirroring her movements. Before long, they were spinning, stopping, darting, and prancing together like partners in some secret dance. Hazel's laughter rang through the air, and Sampson's ears stayed locked on her, eager to copy every step.

When Izzy walked Opal back to her paddock, she paused at the rail, Opal lowering her head immediately to graze without a second glance for her foal. Sampson, older and braver now, had eyes only for Hazel.

Izzy smiled softly. *Look at them,* she thought. *Like they were made for each other.*

Just then, a car pulled into the yard. Hazel's mum and dad stepped out, waving as they came closer. They joined Izzy at the fence, their faces warming as they watched Hazel skipping through the sand with Sampson trotting faithfully at her side.

"She's incredible with him," Hazel's mum whispered.

"It's more than that," Izzy replied. "They have a bond I've never seen before in a young rider and a foal. He trusts her completely."

Hazel's dad folded his arms, eyes shining. "She's dreamed of a horse of her own for as long as she could talk."

Izzy hesitated, then turned to them. "Her birthday's next week, isn't it?"

They nodded.

"Well…" Izzy took a breath. "I've been thinking. I don't need another horse for the show pen. But Hazel and Sampson… they're something special. I'd like to gift him to her — for her birthday."

Hazel's mum's eyes widened, and her dad's jaw dropped. For a long moment, they said nothing, just watching as Hazel dropped into a crouch and Sampson nuzzled her shoulder like a loyal puppy.

Finally, her mum blinked back tears. "Izzy, that's the most incredible gift. She'll never forget this."

Her dad nodded firmly. "She's ready. And she'll work hard to do right by him. We'd be honoured to accept."

TIzzy smiled, relief and joy in her expression. "Then it's settled. But we'll keep it a secret until her birthday. I want it to be the surprise of her life."

Together, they stood by the rail, silent witnesses to the girl and the foal moving as one, both unaware of the life-changing surprise just around the corner.

# Chapter 34

Hazel's birthday was everything she had dreamed of. All her family gathered at the barn, her most favourite place in the world, for a picnic tea amongst the horses. Her friends were there too, their laughter ringing through the yard as they played games and ran between the picnic rugs.

On the table sat a beautiful unicorn cake, its pastel colours sparkling in the sunlight, surrounded by platters of savouries and bowls of treats. Each of Hazel's friends had a party bag waiting for them, filled with little surprises.

Hazel was showered with thoughtful gifts. Huxley handed her a carefully wrapped parcel, his face glowing with pride. Inside was a clay sculpture he had made and painted himself a tiny Sampson, complete with his blaze and belly splash.

Hazel gasped. "Oh, Huxley… I love it! It's perfect!" She hugged him tightly, and her heart swelled at the thoughtfulness of all her friends' presents.

But as the day went on, Hazel noticed something odd. Opal and Sampson's paddock was empty. *Strange,* she thought. *Izzy must be doing something with them.*

Soon it was time for cake. Everyone gathered around as Hazel's friends sang "Happy Birthday" at the top of their lungs. Hazel blew out the candles in one breath, her mum calling out, "Don't forget to make a wish!" The group giggled knowingly — they all guessed what Hazel's wish would be.

And then it happened.

Around the corner came a familiar little face — Sampson, trotting proudly, wearing a brand-new halter and lead rope. A great bow sat around his neck, fluttering as he moved.

Hazel froze, confused. "Sampson?"

Izzy walked alongside him, smiling so wide her eyes shone. She stopped in front of Hazel and gently placed the lead rope in her hand. "Happy birthday, Hazel. He's a gift — for you."

The world tilted. Hazel's mouth dropped open, her voice barely a whisper. "Are you… serious? No jokes?"

Izzy laughed and nodded. "No jokes. He's yours."

Hazel flung her arms around Izzy, then turned and buried her face in Sampson's soft muzzle, her hands trembling with joy. She was speechless, overwhelmed by the dream she had wished for finally coming true.

She looked up, her eyes sweeping across her family and friends. Narni stood at the back, wiping a tear from her cheek, her smile glowing with pride.

After a few moments, Izzy led Opal and Sampson back to their paddock, letting mare and foal rest. Hazel's parents gathered her close, explaining gently, "When he's weaned in a few months, Sampson will officially be yours. Until then, you'll help care for him, learn with him, and lay the foundations for your journey together."

Both sets of grandparents stepped forward with hugs, pressing envelopes into Hazel's hands. Inside were vouchers for special lessons and trainers, chosen so she and Sampson could grow as a team.

"It will be a few years before you ride him," Narni explained kindly, "but there's so much you can do before then. Groundwork, liberty, trust… it's all the foundation for the horse he'll become."

Hazel's eyes shone with tears, her grin stretching from ear to ear. She could hardly believe it. Today, the wish she'd made at every birthday had finally come true. Sampson was hers.

It was, without a doubt, the happiest day of her life.

# Chapter 35

The big day has finally come. Weaning day.

Hazel stood by the rail, her heart thudding as Opal and Sampson were gently led apart. She braced herself for squeals or stamping hooves, but to her surprise, neither mother nor foal seemed the least bit upset.

Opal gave a soft snort, lowered her head, and went straight back to grazing as though she'd been waiting for this moment. Sampson blinked once at her, then turned his nose toward Hazel with a nicker. His little hooves trotted confidently across the yard until he reached her side, pressing his muzzle into her hands.

Izzy chuckled. "Looks like he knows exactly who he belongs with now."

Hazel still couldn't believe it. *He's mine. Officially mine.*

A few months later, Hazel and Aunt Becky saddled up for a quiet trail ride. Becky swung onto Marble's back, the young gelding now calm and steady with more miles under his hooves. Hazel mounted Spartan, his black coat gleaming, and clipped a lead rope to Sampson's halter.

"Just a short ride," Becky reminded, smiling.

"Of course," Hazel said, her voice glowing with pride.

Sampson trotted happily alongside Spartan, his ears pricked, tail swishing with curiosity at every bird call and rustle in the trees. He followed Hazel's cues as though he'd been doing it forever.

When they arrived back at the barn, Hazel spotted movement in the arena. Izzy was riding Opal, the mare's dark coat glistening as she flowed through her paces. Izzy arched her neck, ears flicking happily, as though proud to be back under saddle now that her foal was strong and independent.

Hazel leaned against Spartan's neck, grinning. "Look, Sampson — your mum's back at work too."

Becky smiled as Marble slowed to a halt beside them. "It's good to see them both happy, isn't it?"

Hazel nodded, her heart full. Sampson was hers now, but Opal would always be part of the picture — a reminder of where it all began.

A few months after that, Hazel stood in the round pen for Sampson's very first liberty and long reining lesson. The trainer guided her step by step, showing her how to use her body language, her voice, her hands. To Hazel's delight, Sampson caught on quickly, flicking his ears to her, trotting forward, turning, and stopping when she asked.

"He's a natural," the trainer said. "But then, so are you."

Hazel's cheeks flushed with pride.

That evening, Hazel carried a blanket into Sampson's paddock and spread it across the grass. She sat quietly, watching the sun dip low and the sky blush pink. Sampson wandered over, gave a little neigh, and folded himself down beside her, his warm body pressed close.

Hazel stroked his neck, leaning against him. "We've got so many adventures ahead of us, Sampson. I can't wait."

The colt's breathing slowed, his head resting on the ground. Hazel lay back in the grass, gazing up at the first stars as her best friend drifted to sleep beside her.

And together, they dreamed of all the future might bring.